THE EXILED

A WEB OF LIES: BOOK 1

JASON LEIGH SMITH

Also by Jason Leigh Smith

From the Harvest War Archives

A Web Of Lies
The Exiled
The Allied
The Deceived
The Betrayed (coming soon)

The Vault Worlds
Revelation
Complication (coming soon)

Children of the Revolution
Children of the Revolution

THE
EXILED

ISBN: 978-1-923163-69-0 (Paperback)

A catalogue record for this work is available from the National Library of Australia

Cover Design: Clark & Mackay
Format and Typeset: Clark & Mackay
Published by Jason Leigh Smith and Clark & Mackay

Proudly printed in Australia by Clark & Mackay

Thanks to my family, for the endless patience as I brought these books to life. Mum and Dad, thanks for listening to the countless hours of me talking through plans and story arcs over the past years. Thanks also to Stephen, for putting up with me while I lived in my head, perfecting, perfecting, and perfecting.

THE MOUNTAINBOUND LANDS OF
BELISSIA
CEYLON
IBRASIL
THE CRADLE
DARKWOOD
TANGLEWOOD
TANAH MERAH
RY'ESSOR
BAY OF RYESSOR
EVENWOOD
RY'ETTE
CHANCY
GHOST COUNTRY
EASTERN COUNTY
TRAHDELL
THE BORDER RANGES
SILVER LAKE
NORTHERN COUNTY
RY'OKO
BAY OF TOWERS
SILVERTON
CRESTELL
EZGUARD
RY'DOR
THE COASTAL SWAMPS
PELFAR RIVER
GUSTING
GAVIDGEON
BAY OF GUSTING
GRANVILLE
WESTERN COUNTY
SOUTHERN COUNTY
FARPORT
RY'KYK
FAR BAY
RY'REE

*These books are for the little boy who
built sandcastles on the beach and
dreamed of magic ... we did it.*

1917 A.P.W.

(AFTER PURGE WAR)

PROLOGUE

SELENNA DODGED THE Shadowbeast's attack, her boots sliding for grip on the icy ground. The Shadowbeast, a foul creature that could only be described as an insect as long as she was tall, lunged too wide, leaving itself open for attack. She took the chance, and reaching down into the depths of her being, to the almost-endless well of her roiling mancery, she pulled forth a whisper of her immense power. Selenna then released it as a blast from her outstretched hand, a single tendril of orange energy that tore through the Shadowbeast's hard carapace. Sparks exploded from the impact, and the creature fell dead to the ground, with all its spindly legs twitching in the snow.

Selenna looked at the frozen wasteland around her. Everywhere, the Elves were locked in a furious battle with the Shadowbeasts. Elven mancery blasted here and there, Shadowbeasts shrieked as they attacked, and Elves and beast alike died in droves, so that bodies and blood littered the snow for as far as Selenna could see into the surrounding ice.

'We have to keep up the attack,' said the male Elf beside her.

She turned to look into his serious brown eyes. He had handsome features and pointed ears, 'No, Neroan. We need to find the Necromancer and end this war before more Elves die needlessly.'

The remaining three Inquisitors stepped into place, so that there were two on either side of Selenna, with her at the centre. They were the Inquisitors, the most powerful Elves of their time, each representing the pinnacles of the five schools of Elven mancery: Pyromancy, Aeromancy, Electromancy, Aquamancy, and her own power, Enermancy.

Mystan, the Aquamancer spoke next, 'I do love a good fight, though. I'd be happy to destroy more of those foul beasts before we round up the Necromancer.'

Selenna rounded on him, anger flashing in her golden eyes. 'You fool. Tens of thousands of Belissians have already died in this war. The Councils have tasked us to end it by killing the Necromancer, and so we shall. Come.'

They fell into step beside her, her long strides taking them between two rows of five, black basalt pillars that stood up from the snow. Selenna could see engravings covering every inch of their six-yard height, though she had no idea what it said or who had written them.

Shadowbeasts threw themselves at the five Inquisitors as they strode between the pillars, but the

Elven mancery was far too powerful. The creatures simply fell dead to the ground with gaping wounds. One, its legs twitching as arcs of blue Electromancy danced between them, another with a four-yard long shard of frozen Aquamancy in its insect-like head, and more that had simply been melted by Pyromancy.

Up ahead, the ground rose into a frozen hillock with a door made from the same material as the columns behind her. Guarding the entrance, five Elves, dressed in the shining black armour of a mancer Element, each representing one of the Schools of Mancery. They were formed in the same manner as Selenna and her Inquisitors, though far younger, and so hadn't come into their true power, yet.

'Great Inquisitor,' the Element Sergeant, identifiable by the three pointed arrows above a burning flame emblazoned on his chest saluted by bowing his head and crossing his arms over his breast plate. 'Vylok is trapped in the crypt below. A Mancer Element and a team of Truthseers have him pinned down. He is running out of blood to fuel his Necromancy.'

'We have him,' breathed Neroan, excitement touching his voice.

'The war is over,' nodded the Element Sergeant.

Unwilling to admit victory until Vylok was dead, Selenna said, 'Take us to him. It's time to end this war.'

1967 A.P.W.

(AFTER PURGE WAR)

CHAPTER ONE

CID

CAPTAIN SELOUTEAU DROPPED the short distance from the wood deck of her airship to the soft, moist ground below. It was a bright night above, but little light penetrated through the rainforest's layers.

She lit a glowstone and held it out before her, shining the palm-sized stone in a circular motion that lit the surrounding undergrowth and her face with a purple hue. Like all Elves, she was tall and muscular with broad shoulders, and like her mother, Selouteau had strong features and hard, golden brown eyes.

The forest loomed like a wall of darkness around her, broken only by the twittering of night larks and thrumming of insects, and despite the late hour, the warm air was thick and hard to breathe.

She took a squelching step forward.

'How do you expect to sneak into the Human camp if you make that much noise whenever you move?' said the Truthseer from behind her.

Selouteau turned to face the lithe male Elf as he dropped to the ground at her side. 'Ensign Perch, perhaps if you had stayed with the Truthseers, you could have learned to read their minds from here, and save us walking through this stinking mess.'

She flicked some muck from one of her shining black boots.

'We both know I'm much better off with you in the Armada than in the Great Library, wasting my life as a Truthseer,' said Perch.

'True. And I can't deny having a Truthseer onboard is helpful,' she said.

Selouteau motioned for him to follow as she set off between the trees. As much as she hated the heat, the stifling air and how the forest floor clung to her silvery uniform, she was happy to be away from the capital Evenwood and the Councils' constant debates.

Walking beside her, Perch patted the twin swords crossing his back and the utility pouches surrounding his hips. He then smoothed his tight leather jerkin before he spoke: 'I know you still think about your mother, Selouteau.'

Her chest tightened, but she continued walking, pretending that it hadn't affected her. She should have known better; there was no escaping the Truthseer's prying mind. He was young and enigmatic, but still a Truthseer.

Selouteau knew that Ensign Perch couldn't bend one of the five elements to his will with mancery—unlike the majority of the Elven population—but instead had been trained by the Truthseers in the art of reading and controlling the mind. Secluded in the halls of the Great Library, Perch had dedicated his life to the Elven Truthseers, until the arrival of the Humans—just six weeks ago—when he had begged to join Selouteau's crew.

In the short time since Perch had enlisted, she had found his abilities useful.

The Truthseer continued: 'Selenna was the greatest Inquisitor in memory, and the Councils reported that she alone ended the Necromancer's War and brought peace to Belissia. I know she'd be proud to see how far her daughter has come—'

'It still would have been nice to have a body to mourn … Knowing that none of the Inquisitors' bodies were recovered—or Vylok's for that matter—is disconcerting.'

Stepping over a knot of twisted roots, covered in lichen, she watched him consider her statement. He still hadn't responded as they made their way between the towering fig and cedar trees, their trunks standing like moss-covered sentinels in the darkness.

Finally he replied: 'The Inquisitors were the only Elves granted the power of controlling *shifting*. And Vylok could move in and out of the Shadow Realm as he pleased. Their final battle could have taken place anywhere, Selouteau. Anywhere.'

She let the weight of his comment sink in. Knowledge of the Inquisitors' ability to control portals through *shifting* was known only to the highest of the Elven hierarchy. She had only learned about it through her mother, the Great Inquisitor. The fact that the Truthseer knew about it troubled her.

'And even if the Councils did find the final battle site,' Perch continued, 'there's little chance their bodies remained. The Inquisitors were the most powerful Elves of their time, Selouteau ... I don't think any Elf alive could rival your mother in battle. I doubt there'd be much left to find.'

'It still feels unfinished,' said Selouteau.

'It's been fifty years since Vylok was defeated by your mother and the Inquisitors. Wouldn't she have returned to you if she could?' Perch reached out to rest his hand on one of her broad, armoured shoulders. 'Elves live long lives, Selouteau. Spending the next few centuries questioning the Councils—'

'I wasn't questioning the Councils,' Selouteau said firmly. She shrugged off his hand and continued through the undergrowth, the smell of rotting wood thick in her nose.

For a time, they continued without speaking, and Selouteau took the moments to enjoy the sounds of the dense tropical forest around them: the buzzing insects, the hoots of the night larks and the rustle of small predators moving through the undergrowth.

'Is it tiresome being a Truthseer, always reading everyone's thoughts?' said Selouteau.

'It's not always. We can dampen the speed and loudness of the thoughts, and Truthseeing isn't foolproof.'

Selouteau was unsure what he meant, but knew she didn't want to ask any further. Though not used in the military as soldiers, the Truthseers played a pivotal role with the Elven hierarchy: they were employed as spies, and to preside over meetings and to root out the Truth, always. Their power was said to be infallible …

Selouteau continued leading them east, through the region known as the Western County: a deep, broad valley, full of thick forests and humid air. Every surface she touched or pushed past was wet. Leaves, trunks and hanging vines left streaks of moisture across her back, so it wasn't long before the uniform beneath her armour was several shades darker.

They followed the natural rise of the land, until a precipice fell away to the darkened forests on their right. They continued up the jagged edge all the way until they topped the valley's rim and trailed the escarpment south. Before long and after brushing through the last few layers of forest, Selouteau found herself standing on a tall spit of land, jutting into the calm waters of the Southern Ocean.

A breeze wafted lazily over them; the flow of air evaporating the moisture from her uniform left her skin cold and clammy. Selouteau took a deep breath: the smell of salt and fish on the air. To her right sprawled the valley of the Western County from where they had climbed, and to the left, their destination. She pocketed the glowstone and produced a longscope in unison with Perch.

In a vast semicircle of cliffs, approximately one league in diameter, was the Human camp of Gusting, though the term 'camp' hardly seemed appropriate; it could easily be described as a fortified town.

Lanterns dotted the palisade wall that surrounded a still-under-construction stone perimeter. The town itself was full of low, square buildings lit from within and arranged in neat rows that continued down to the sandy beach, where a jetty poked into the calm water of the cove. A small fleet of Human airships bobbed several yards above the moonlit water, their decks silent and unmoving. Selouteau eyed the vessels. They were ugly creations, full of sharp angles and dark colours—nothing like the work of art that was each Elven airship.

She closed the longscope with a snap. Gusting's position was brilliantly defensible. Built within the cliffs, it would be hard to attack from the north and east, the dense rainforests of the Western County slowed any approach from the west, and the airships guarded the cliff-walled harbour.

'What's your assessment, Ensign?' She arched an eyebrow.

Tendrils of his blond hair danced around his long, pointed ears as he lowered his longscope.

'It's those two gun emplacements that worry me,' he said, pointing across the distance to the north and south of Gusting. 'They are large enough to take down an airship—so I'm glad you chose to land far from here—but I see no evidence of the Ambassador's ship. We'd need to wait for daylight to conduct a proper search. We're also too far from the town itself for my Truthseeing.'

'We're not here for the ship … How close do you need to be to sense the Ambassador?'

'I'd need to be inside the walls to confirm if he still lives,' he said.

Selouteau watched as the Truthseer's brows furrowed in thought, and an unusual sincerity entered his expression.

'Do you think we'll make it in and out alive, Selouteau?' he asked.

Selouteau looked past Perch and Gusting, out to the east, where the twin suns would be rising soon. 'We're Elves, Ensign Perch. Of course we'll get out alive. As discussed, I'll cause enough distraction for you to infiltrate the camp, locate and retrieve the Ambassador and get out. Keep your Truthseeing open and call for help if you need. And Ensign, I know you're only new to my team, but the correct form of address is Captain or Ma'am,' said Selouteau.

She held his gaze long enough to make the point clear. Then taking off at a jog, she followed the cliff edge further east.

According to reports, the Humans had landed six weeks ago on the beaches here in the south of Belissia. They were spotted by an Elven airship on patrol before the Councils lost contact with the crew. Without the wreckage to prove the patrol had been shot down by the Humans, the Elven Councils— ever diplomatic—sent an Ambassador. A week had since passed, and Selouteau knew the Councils had lost contact with him shortly after he reported safe arrival in Gusting. So, without sufficient evidence, the Elven Councils were forced to send a search party to shed light on the situation: namely, her.

As far as Selouteau was concerned, unsanctioned landings on Elven soil and two unprovoked attacks could only mean war, even if the Councils wouldn't admit it.

'*Captain?*' Perch's voice reverberated inside her head.

'Yes, Ensign?' Selouteau replied out loud as she jogged across the uneven surface atop the cliffs.

'*I'm checking our link … Can you hear me?*'

'*Obviously,*' she spoke through her mind, into his Truthseeing link.

'*Excellent.*'

Slowing to a walk, Selouteau edged to the sharp precipice and looked down to the wooded hills, hundreds of yards below. With her mancery, there was no need to climb, but she still needed to be quick. She was due north of Gusting and approximately a one-half league from the defenders: far enough to have distance on her side, but close enough that she could still be seen, especially at night.

She reached with her mind, down to where she felt the deep well of her roiling power. Grasping her Enermancy, she released a trickle. The familiar warmth flowed up her torso, down through her arms and into her long slender fingers. Her hands began to glow with a purple hue.

A sphere of energy materialised above her hands that continued to expand until it was the width of her shoulders, with patterns rippling across its surface. She lowered it over the cliff and stepped onto it; the Enermancy bent under her weight, but it was far stronger than what was necessary to hold her. Raising her arms, palms facing the silvery moonlit clouds, Selouteau descended the cliff face on the cushion of her power.

Lowering herself quickly, lest she be seen, Selouteau saw the purple light dance along the stone behind her as she came to rest on the sandy soil. Coarse grains squeaked under her heel, and with a quick scan, she surveyed the area. Nothing moved.

Running through the plan in her mind, Selouteau created seven additional spheres of Enermancy that bobbed in the air around her. She allowed herself a moment to consider the destruction she was about to wreak; though she enjoyed the violent explosions her mancery created—and was quite capable of using her power to kill—her mission was to extract the Ambassador and to not start a war. She was the daughter of the Grand Admiral and the Great Inquisitor; she had a legacy to live up to.

With the halo of glowing spheres floating around her, Selouteau nodded; she would do what had to be done.

Through their Truthseeing link, Selouteau could tell that Ensign Perch had already scaled the cliffs and was running through the sandy woods towards Gusting. She could sense how he moved—like a predator from the Rift—and she could feel his emotions too. As he leapt over a low stand of brush, Selouteau felt his swell of excitement like it was her own. She took a moment to feel how his Truthseeing searched the land ahead for any hidden scouts; he'd sense them long before they heard him move. She smiled with him as he slid over a felled tree and vaulted down the following embankment. He was trading speed for silence—and enjoying it.

Selouteau breathed heavily with Perch as he skidded to a stop and took a moment to control his breathing. Crouching in the shadow of a low tree, he peered at the clearway surrounding Gusting's defences. She saw as he pinpointed the positions of the patrolling soldiers, the thuds of their steps falling across the palisade walls. She felt him slide two small throwing knives from his right thigh. And like a statue, he waited for her promised distraction.

Opening her eyes to lessen the strength of their connection, Selouteau moved to where she could see Gusting. She stood atop a small rise to the north, and from her elevated position, she could see the unsuspecting soldiers exactly where Perch had shown her. Picking a point to minimise casualties, she spoke into their link: *'I'm ready.'*

She lobbed two spheres of Enermancy at the defences of Gusting. The purple missiles streaked across the dark expanse before smashing into the bottom of the palisade wall. The detonations blew splinters of wood into the night sky, and the noise clapped like the thunder from a Western County summer storm.

Selouteau directed two more spheres towards Gusting with a flick of her wrist, and a second round of explosions tore into the wooden defences. An alarm bell started wailing through the thick night air. Shouted commands of soldiers preparing themselves for battle joined the din, though the Humans spoke in a language she didn't understand. Selouteau guided another two missiles down through the clouds of dust that had been lifted by her explosions.

Across the bay, Selouteau felt Perch surge to his feet and hurl the knives with deadly accuracy. The blades skewered two wall-mounted lanterns and killed their light. Darting across the sandy clearway and toward the darkened wall, the Truthseer then took a running leap.

Selouteau felt his strength and speed, as—with deft hands—the Truthseer topped the wall and slipped into the compound beyond. Landing, he rolled into the darkness behind some packing crates where she felt him spread his Truthseeing—a sensation that still felt strange to her—to scour the surrounding buildings with his mind.

'I've found him, but he's injured, Captain. We need to hurry,' said Perch to Selouteau's mind.

Distracted by their connection, Selouteau failed to notice the Human defenders that had found her. The two cannons Perch had spotted earlier opened fire. A white explosion landed at her feet with such force that it lifted her into the air and threw her down the next sand dune. Air rushed from her lungs. And as she fell across the soft ground, the superheated sand fell like broken glass around her.

With her long Elven ears ringing from the explosion, Selouteau spoke into their connection, *'Ensign Perch, they're using energy-based weapons, which means I can use it against them.'*

She pulled herself to her feet and looked over the top of the dune, hoping it had been a lucky shot. But it wasn't. The cannons opened fire again, and more white explosions smashed into the ground around her. Ducking and weaving through the crossfire, she cast her last two spheres of Enermancy and was rewarded with more satisfying explosions. Selouteau felt a sudden grin spread across her lips. She was enjoying this.

Breath gushed from her lungs as another shot hit her, throwing her up and over the dune. Sliding to a stop behind the rolling dunes of sand, Selouteau examined her arm and groaned. *Perhaps they weren't just lucky shots*, she thought. The gunfire had hit her just below the shoulders of her armour, charring her unprotected grey uniform and skin together into one stinking mess.

The smell of burnt flesh and melted clothing filled her nose. She closed her eyes and reached around to poke at the wound. Pain lanced up her arm and across her chest. 'Only minor …' she said, as the dark of unconsciousness enveloped her.

CHAPTER TWO

THE DIMLY LIT streets of Gusting's interior allowed Perch an easy path, and Selouteau's rain of missiles ensured the Humans' attention remained focused away from him. Hiding as a group of soldiers ran past, their officer shouting orders in a language he didn't know, Perch allowed their waves of fear to wash over him. He drank in the emotion—it invigorated him.

The Ambassador needed his help urgently, but for now, he focused on avoiding the enemy. Shifting from shadow to shadow, Perch weaved around the soldiers amassing in the main square. He followed the captive Elf's weak thoughts as they led him toward the largest building in Gusting: a two-storey structure that looked unfinished in its construction.

Circling around the imposing building, Perch moved down an unlit alley and, with a swift kick, brought down a wooden door. With a sword in one hand and a dagger in the other, he stalked into the brightly lit corridor beyond.

'*I'm in,*' he relayed to Selouteau, as he mentally scanned the corridors ahead.

From the floor above, shouts caught his attention. The language seemed … simple and barbaric, not at all like their musical Elven language. His long Elven ears twitched, and he smirked when he heard how the orders were bellowed in rage—Selouteau's onslaught was keeping them busy.

Pushing his mind farther into the building, Perch found the Ambassador down in the lowest levels: the dungeon. He took a step forward, but a group of Human soldiers rounded the corner ahead. It was the first time he'd seen the Humans so close. They didn't look like much: shorter and stockier than Elves, they had pale skin and wore dark green, plated armour.

For a moment, the men stopped and stared. Perch could see their thoughts, and although he didn't understand their language, he understood their confusion and fear. Taking advantage, he attacked.

Perch threw two daggers at the closest soldiers, who fell with the blades jutting from their twitching eyes. Barrelling into another three before they raised their strange weapons, Perch opened their throats wide with his sword.

Blood sprayed across the white-painted walls as he spun from the attack, and carrying his momentum forward, he kicked out as hard as he could. His leather boot connected with the last soldier's chest and sent him sprawling into the closest wall. The sound of bones crunching followed, and without a moment's hesitation, Perch ended the broken man's life with a swift jab to the heart; better to ease the Human's death than allow him to suffer.

Moving fast now that he had left evidence of his presence, Perch darted farther into the building, down a flight of stairs into an area that had been dug straight into the sandy soil. Through a corridor and into a row of caged cells, where he followed the wafting scent of an unwashed body to the last cell. He kicked at the wooden door with his boot until the timber splintered and fell to pieces.

He stepped into the cell, and a nauseating smell filled his nostrils: a combination of faeces, grime and decaying matter. Fighting the urge to vomit, Perch called, 'Ambassador Tendallanon?'

A groan came from the darkest corner, and with his Truthseeing, Perch could feel just how weak the Elf was; he would have to retrieve the Ambassador and carry him. Taking a deep breath from the hallway, Perch moved forward into the stinking cell.

Soft straw littered the floor, and Perch tried not to think about how it squelched under his boots. He crouched and felt along the Ambassador's naked, clammy body with a methodical precision. The Elf's back was puckered into large weeping welts, and as he touched one, the Ambassador whimpered.

Thoughts then filtered across Perch's mind from the Ambassador: '*Leave.*'

'You're going to be alright, Ambassador Tendallanon,' said Perch, relaying calming reassurance through his Truthseeing. 'I am Ensign Perch of Captain Selouteau's crew. We are here to rescue you.'

Careful to preserve the Ambassador's modesty, Perch probed the remaining parts of his body. He felt deep lacerations on both wrists and ankles: obvious signs of restraints, yet so deep that Perch thought the Humans must have hung him by his hands.

Across his back, the long welts oozed fluid; pus or blood, he could not tell in the darkened cell. A badly swollen face, with both eyes closed and puffy, and a nose deformed from its usual regal shape. As best Perch could tell in the unlit darkness, the Elf would soon die of blood loss and malnutrition.

'They're coming,' said the Ambassador feebly.

Perch flashed his mind out to the building above and around them, searching for who the Ambassador warned against, but aside from those in the upper floors still screeching orders, he felt nothing.

'*Captain,*' said Perch as he pushed his mind across the connection, '*Captain, I have Ambassador Tendallanon but will need cover for an extraction. I'm in the largest building to the southwest of the compound.*'

No response came.

Perch shouted into the link, '*Captain!*'

Outside the fort of Gusting, Selouteau startled awake. The first thing she noticed was Perch's voice echoing around her mind. The second was the pain in her arm. She cursed. She must have blacked out, but for how long, she couldn't tell.

'*Captain!*' Perch repeated himself through the link.

'Yes, I'm here,' groaned Selouteau as she sat upright, careful to not aggravate her damaged arm. She examined the sand dunes around her. She had landed in a depression that had saved her from most of the fire, but not by much. The ground around her was littered with little specks of glass that twinkled in the moonlight.

'*I said I'm in the largest—*'

'Yes, I heard you.' Selouteau rubbed at temple with her good hand.

'*Captain … he's dying. We need to hurry.*'

'Understood, Ensign. I'm coming.'

Selouteau cursed again. She was happy Ambassador Tendallanon was alive, but having him incapacitated made things considerably more difficult. Favouring her good arm, she peered over the sandy rise and ducked as the cannons renewed their steady thumping. After the first shots flew wide, the gunners adjusted their aim. Streamers of white energy tracked to her position, and hot glass exploded wherever it hit the sand.

It was time to use their energy against them.

With her undamaged arm, Selouteau summoned another sphere of Enermancy around her and hardened the barrier to form a reflective surface. She then stepped into the line of fire.

White energy pounded the shield, and with each shot, her mancery danced and rippled in purple waves. Though muffled, the drumming deafened her.

'I *can* use their energy,' she said with a laugh.

She conjured another ball of Enermancy and used it like a sponge to absorb the oncoming cannon fire. More and more shots were collected and trapped within her power, so the orb grew brighter with each passing second, until it was so bright it showered the surrounding dunes in brilliance.

Selouteau had never controlled this much energy before, and she could feel the pressure quickly draining her. Sweat poured from her face and down her back, but the cannons kept firing; she needed to act, so she hefted the ball of energy with a grunt and tossed it at Gusting.

The sphere flew in an arc that cast strange shadows on the surrounding landscape. And as it neared the fortified walls, Selouteau saw the small army of Humans gathered on the walls and streets of Gusting. As one, the soldiers stopped and turned to stare—open-mouthed—at the descending sphere. And at the last moment before impact, Selouteau looked away.

Intense white light dissipated every shadow, and to the east, Selouteau saw the gutted remains of the Ambassador's airship. It was black and ruined, straddling a dune with all of its flight surfaces burnt to a crisp. She felt a twinge of sadness; this and the Ambassador's state was the evidence the Councils needed. There had to be war.

Her thoughts shattered with the booming explosion that tore through the night. The shock-wave shoved her backwards.

Then came a dark silence.

With ears ringing and her eyes adjusting, Selouteau called out: 'Ensign Perch, can you hear me?'

'*Captain, what did you do?*' came the Truthseer's reply. '*The ground is still shaking.*'

With a sigh of relief, Selouteau surveyed the destruction. The closest cannon lay in ruins, and with it large portions of the northern and eastern walls. Whole rows of the low square houses had been reduced to rubble, and scores of the soldiers had simply vanished. In their place, a crater—eighty yards in diameter—sat charred and smoking. Flaming debris floated in the sky, and as Selouteau watched, pools of white fire caught onto the remaining structures and began to spread, burning and melting everything it touched.

'Ensign, don't go anywhere near the white flames. They're even burning through the stone,' said Selouteau.

'*Understood… and Captain,*' said the Truthseer, and through their link, Selouteau could feel him struggling with his words, '*the Ambassador…*'

'Hold tight, Ensign, I'll be there as soon as I can.'

The Humans sounded an alarm that Selouteau thought must mean retreat: they raced between the growing fires and collapsing buildings and fled for the beach. She paused to watch their escape down to the cove's silvery waters, as above them, foreboding shapes caught her attention. She saw twelve—no, fifteen—airships gliding into the fire-lit haze surrounding Gusting.

'Ensign?' The word fell from her open mouth. 'Ensign Perch, we need to retreat! A fleet of Human airships is approaching fast. They'll make landfall in minutes.'

'*I'll have to carry him.*'

Cursing, Selouteau released her protective bubble of Enermancy. It fizzled out of existence, and immediately, the first waves of the *sickness* hit her. Her vision swam, her mind reeled, and she swayed on her feet—she took a moment to steady herself. She knew this was the price she must pay for using that much mancery in so short a time. She had no choice. There was no cure, and no escaping the sickness. She just had to push through it.

With her head throbbing, Selouteau picked her way down the dune. Rubble and flame littered the area, chunks scattered as far as she could see into the night. Hurrying around the clumps of shattered wall and fighting the beginning of a piercing headache, she crossed over the remains of Gusting's defences.

She was drenched in sweat—her silvery uniform long since turned a dark grey beneath the plates of her golden armour. Selouteau skirted the still smoking crater and hastened to where she sensed Perch through their link. Everywhere, broken bodies were tossed asunder, limbs askew at strange angles and blood splattered across the surrounding debris. Selouteau felt no remorse or malice toward the dead. Like her, they were soldiers. And like her, they followed orders.

She wondered if their orders came from Councils like her own—consistently out of touch with their world. Could this escalation have been avoided if the Councils had acted sooner or if they'd attempted further diplomacy? As much as she wanted the answer to be yes, Selouteau knew it was unlikely. The Humans had shot down an Elven scout ship, gutted the Ambassador's ship and tortured the Elf to the point of death—they came with intent.

What that intent meant for the future, she didn't know. And right now, she didn't need to know, as her duty was to ensure the Ambassador's safe escape. The Ambassador could tell the Councils why the Humans were here. Vital information, especially if this incident started another Belissian war.

Squeezing the bridge of her nose against the sickness, Selouteau stopped to observe the pale flames before her. The level of devastation was unlike anything she'd had ever seen. As far as she knew, no Pyromancer had ever produced anything similar, and unlike regular mancery, the white fires attacked every surface with utter destructiveness. Selouteau covered her face as a nearby house collapsed on melting foundations and showered her with heat. Flurries of bright embers erupted upwards and danced into the night.

She hastened to find Perch. If she could get this information and the Ambassador back to the Councils; perhaps they could find a better way to combat the Human energy weapons. She hoped so.

Checking her bearings in relation to the approaching airships, Selouteau hurried down an intact alley. She staggered under another wave of sickness and concentrated on Perch's link to guide her. Tripping as she rounded the last corner, she caught herself on the wall of a building and breathed through the pain.

'Captain?' Perch called.

Slowly, she looked up from the stone wall to see Perch approaching, a body tightly wrapped in a blanket thrown over his shoulder.

'Ensign, I'm fine.' She held up her good hand. 'I just need a moment … The sickness is particularly strong tonight.'

'I'd say,' he said with a chuckle, surveying the surrounding devastation. 'Considering the mess you've left, I'm surprised it's not *you* over my shoulder.'

She managed an unconvincing grimace. 'How is he?'

Perch shook his head. 'He's lost a lot of blood. We need to move … Here, let me help.' Perch reached forward to place a soft hand over her face. Immediately the weight of her sickness reduced to a dull throb; the pain slackened, her back straightened, and her nausea washed away.

'Whoa,' said Perch, sagging at the knees and catching himself on the same wall as Selouteau. 'I only meant to take some of the pain.'

'That was only a fraction of my sickness,' said Selouteau, teasingly. 'No wonder you didn't make it as a mancer.'

'That is unnecessarily unkind of you, Captain,' said Perch. And gritting his teeth, he hefted the Ambassador over his shoulder again.

Feeling markedly better, Selouteau stood tall and guided the ensign away from the beach, towards the northwestern walls. She checked over her shoulder to where the rising smoke obscured much of the cliff-walled harbour. 'Those airships should have made landfall by now. We have to escape before the Humans come back in force.'

They hurried through the rows of buildings, as the thick, choking smoke wafted through the streets before them. It was filled with embers that swirled around the structures and obscured her view in every direction. But she knew where she was going, and in Truth, the haze would help their escape.

Her long ears twitched, as shouting and the steady beat of marching soldiers echoed up from the beach. They were coming.

Quickening her steps, Selouteau rounded another corner, and before them stood the towering northern end of the western wall. She gazed up at the six yard high stone barrier.

'I don't think I'll make it over the wall,' Perch mumbled. 'Go on without me.'

'Don't be so dramatic.'

Directing the Truthseer—who was still carrying the Ambassador—to a nearby building, where he leaned against the timber, Selouteau turned and shook her head: the sickness following tonight's outlay would be legendary. She wasn't looking forward to it.

Using her Enermancy like a blade, Selouteau pushed it slowly into and through the wall until she'd cut a large, circular hole in the stone that fell to the ground with a thud. Together, the Elves clambered through the opening, and still carrying the Ambassador, they fled into the dark, smoky forest.

It didn't take them long to climb up from the cove to the spit of land that jutted out into the calm Southern Ocean. Reaching the top, Selouteau took a deep breath and examined the white fires engulfing the Human fortifications. The melting buildings spewed towers of black smoke that were set against the backdrop of the brightening dawn—the twin suns not yet visible on the horizon.

Pulling herself from the view, she knelt to check Ambassador Tendallanon's faint, irregular pulse. Their mission wasn't over yet.

'Captain.' Perch's tone drew her attention.

She looked to where he was pointing. There on the beach, unobscured by the rising haze, fifteen Human airships unloaded their cargo.

'There are thousands of them …' Perch fought for words. 'It's—'

'It's an invasion.'

CHAPTER THREE

CIƆ

SELOUTEAU SWUNG HER thin sword in a graceful arc. It had been two weeks since her cannon injury at Gusting, but her shoulder felt fully restored, thanks to her healer's expertise.

With deliberate motions, her bare feet slid across the airship's polished wooden deck, as the cool morning wind teased her long black hair.

The duelling sword descended slowly across her torso, before she spun and lowered herself to one knee, blade extending in a jab. Then coming to her feet and standing to attention, Selouteau let the weapon dip. *Perhaps one more time.*

Again, focusing her attention and settling her broad shoulders, Selouteau began her morning Kuaru regimen anew. Flowing from stance to stance, she moved with practised grace—just as she'd been taught. The sword became an extension of her being, scribing careful arcs around her body as she moved. Enacting a complex fight sequence—slowly—Selouteau lengthened each manoeuvre into long, marked motions.

Accentuating balance, strength and control was important in all aspects of her life.

'Captain,' said a voice from across the deck.

Selouteau paused at the interruption. The day had begun without her. Lowering her blade but not looking at the approaching Elf, she took a moment to gaze over the railing of her ship. They floated thousands of yards over the waking world, roughly a half-day's flight from the Elven capital of Evenwood. One-third of the way from Belissia's north to south length, somewhere near the Border Ranges, they were holding position: waiting for orders.

At their current altitude, Selouteau could see some of the continent laid out before her, a mish-mash of colours that looked like a Lesser Races' patchwork quilt. Far to the east, across the rolling Blue Plains of central Belissia, the twin suns peeked above the horizon. Selouteau knew beyond the plains there would be the dark swamps that lined the Belissian coastline, and the calm ocean farther still, but they were lost in the distance, even from their altitude. Selouteau took a deep breath, relishing that second to enjoy the beauty of the day's first golden rays piercing the soft, silvery clouds.

'Good morning, Lieutenant Marillia. Another fine day ahead of us. I trust your pre-dawn watch passed uneventfully?'

'Of course, Captain,' said the younger, shorter Elf, as she bowed her head and smiled. 'May I say, your Kuaru regimen seems perfect this morning.'

Selouteau examined the Lieutenant thoughtfully. It was true that she pushed herself for perfection in everything she did, but rarely did she achieve it, as far as she was concerned. 'There is always room for improvement, though … What is it you wanted, Lieutenant?'

'There is a communication for you from the Grand Admiral Synnathril,' said the Lieutenant.

'I'll take it in my quarters,' said Selouteau.

Turning away, Selouteau padded across the deck with her bare feet. She passed under the wheelhouse and descended into the vessel's aft. Entering her quarters, she placed the sword beside the entrance and approached what was the centrepiece of her small room: a standing desk carved from the tall pines of the Northern County. It was covered in maps, compasses and other cartographic paraphernalia, and atop all that sat a blue globe, perched on a bronze pedestal. Several rings of polished metal encircled the fist-sized artefact, and reaching forward, Selouteau twisted the knobs that adjusted their position. The hazy innards followed the metal rings in a swirling pattern as she adjusted them to the correct positions.

Globe Communicators—or Globcomms, as they were affectionately known—allowed instant communication across the broadest expanses, and by setting the rings to a specific combination, she could connect this one to any other globe on the same sequence. Elves used them to communicate from the farthest reaches of Belissia in an instant. They were crucial for the passage of information, especially when the majority of the Elven population was spread between thousands of Elven Armada airships.

'Captain Selouteau,' said a deep masculine voice that filled her quarters with its resonance.

'Grand Admiral Synnathril,' said Selouteau.

'Please, call me Syn.'

'And you know you can call me Selouteau.'

She could hear the smile in his voice. 'Can I call you daughter?'

'I suppose that depends on who is listening.'

He laughed, and she could picture in her mind the honest smile creasing his gaunt features. 'How is your shoulder?'

'Grand Admiral ... Dad, my onboard healer is exceptional. He fixed the cannon wound within hours. It's been two weeks since the attack on Gusting. My shoulder is fine.'

'And how is the healer, Lieutenant Wreada-llanon? The loss of his brother, Ambassador Tendallanon, must still be difficult.'

'The Truthseers cleared him for active duty, but I do keep a watchful eye on him. I've asked Ensign Perch to provide regular ...' she considered her next words carefully, 'non-invasive updates via Truthseeing. Dad, the loss of the Ambassador was a terrible turn of events. If only we had—'

Her father's deep, commanding voice cut her off, and the Globcomm's smoky innards twisted angrily in response, 'No, Selouteau. Your actions ensured Gusting was not a complete loss. Taking Ensign Perch with you meant he extracted memories from the Ambassador before his death. That was able to provide us more information about the Human language and share that the Humans are following a religious crusade on behalf of their Divine-King. All invaluable insights. Furthermore, your reports from Gusting were paramount in organising the Elven defences. Had the Councils elected to move faster, we might have stopped the Humans before they gained a foothold. As it stands, their ability to construct the powerful white energy weapons you encountered guarantees their beachhead for the time being. This is not your mistake, Selouteau. Do not wear it as such.'

Selouteau couldn't find the words to relay her feelings. She'd spent her entire career trying to live up to the expectations of her parents' successes and couldn't help but feel that Gusting was a failure. Her failure.

'What do the Councils think?' she asked, deflecting his focus.

'The Councils continue to discuss which avenue the Humans may take, as in the two weeks since the apparent invasion, they've not made any radical movements. The Traditionalists still believe that threats and displays of our strength will produce the desired results.'

'And the Integrists?' said Selouteau, thinking of the political movement that rose in the aftermath of the Necromancer's War. They opposed the incumbent Councils' views and believed the Lesser Races should be supported rather than ruled.

'We don't yet have the numbers to vote on change, Selouteau. The reality is, we need more supporters, and we need more seats on the Councils. I'd thought all the needless deaths in the Necromancer's War would have swayed more to our cause ...'

Syn trailed off. Selouteau knew that he was thinking about her mother, Selenna, and how she died to end the Necromancer's War. A sadness welled in her heart, but she smothered it. It had been half a century since her mother's death. She knew her father still mourned, but if she was being honest with herself, she wasn't ready to discuss it with him either. She forced her mind away. If the Humans brokered alliances with the Lesser Races and provoked the rising anti-Elven propaganda, the effects could be devastating. The Traditionalists would want to respond with force, and the Integrists would try to block them. Syn was right to be concerned.

'Who do you think the Humans will target first?' asked Selouteau.

'Our spies reported the Southern Port Masters have already signed treaties with the Humans, and the Islander Port Cities have promised them exclusive trading rights.'

Selouteau focused on the maps laid before her and traced one long finger down Belissia's eastern coastline. She paused on the lowest three of seven dots portraying the Islander Port Cities: 'Dad, the Islanders are traders with nothing more than their seaships floating up and down the coast. They have no armies. Is their defection any great loss to us?'

'Don't be so narrow-minded, Selouteau. There are broader considerations than just military might. The Islanders are the root of all trade in Belissia. Their defection will trigger repercussions, and while it may seem petty to us, the defectors have renamed their ports to Ry'Dor, Ry'Ryk and Ry'Ree.' He was careful to pronounce each name with its new emphasis.

'They're breaking tradition,' said Selouteau, as she summoned her memory of the yellow-eyed, dark-skinned merchant race. 'Do I remember correctly that the original names mean "the home of" the Islander family that controls the port? But the new emphasis changes the meaning to … "owned by"?'

'The Southern Port Masters haven't just changed the ports' names, Selouteau, they have completely taken over. They're imposing higher trade tariffs on all Islanders not aligned with the treaty. And they've promised to keep the tariffs in place until every Port Master signs.'

'Fighting between the Port Cities is hardly new. The Northern and Southern Islanders have always squabbled, and it's not our place to stop them from changing their ports' names.' She struggled to keep the scepticism from her voice.

'Selouteau, this split in the Islander nation will spread to the other races. The Northern Islanders, the Ez, perhaps the Swarmen, and of course the Elves, will be forced to pay more as prices rise. This signing by the Southern Port Cities has destabilised a large portion of Belissian trade.'

'Do you think the Northerner Islanders will put aside old differences and join the Southerners?'

'The Northern Port Cities have always been more lenient towards the other races of Belissia, due largely to their strong trade links with us and the Ez. I think for the time being they will remain. But, Selouteau …' she could hear him thinking through his pause, 'I have also heard reports that the Ez have been contacted by the Humans as well.'

'The Ez?' Her mouth went dry. 'After what we did to them during the Necromancer's War, they're sure to join an anti-Elven movement.'

'I need you to contact the Prince of the Ez. Convince him to allow us an audience with his father, the King of the Ez. And, Selouteau, I need your utmost discretion on this. This order comes from myself. The Councils have no input or knowledge at this stage.'

What?

'Dad, why are you moving behind the Councils' backs? And more to the point, why aren't the Councils talking to the Ez King themselves?'

The tension in his hushed words indicated he was disclosing secret information. 'The Ez are no longer communicating with the Elven Councils.'

The words hit Selouteau like a physical blow. Her head swam, and her mind reeled. For better or worse, the Elves have maintained control of Belissia for nearly two thousand years, but the history of the Traditionalist methods was beginning to work against them. If the Southern Islanders and the Ez sided with the Humans against the Elves, not only was war a certainty, but it would be costly as well.

After rescuing the Ambassador, Selouteau had expected the Humans to march from Gusting with thousands of soldiers. She'd relished the chance to test her military cunning against anything they could offer. But instead, the Humans built defences and waited, like coiled swamp raptors poised to strike. Whispering to traders in underhanded treaties and brokering deals with the Ez hinted at a war she was not equipped to fight; politics, manipulation and economics were not her strengths.

'What makes you think the Prince of the Ez will speak to me?' said Selouteau.

'I am told the Prince has an appreciation of the Elves, particularly the Integrists and their move away from Traditionalist control. He is somewhat disenfranchised from his father's decisions regarding the Humans and has gone into self-imposed exile.'

'How can an exiled Prince help us?' said Selouteau.

'His exile is a political move, Selouteau, one designed to create a public outcry. I hardly think it's permanent. Find him and get me an audience with the King of the Ez.'

'And you know where the Prince is hiding?'

'I will read you the coordinates now.'

Grabbing a stylus, she marked down numbers, as her father's voice echoed out from the blue swirls of the Globcomm. When the stormy innards slowed and the communication disconnected, Selouteau tapped a foot against the timber floor. There was so much to think about.

Her father, Grand Admiral Synnathril of the Elven Armada, head of the entire Elven military, had just asked her to act without the Councils' approval. If discovered, her act would be branded treasonous, a crime punishable as the highest possible offence. Yes, she felt disconnected from the Councils' Traditionalist direction, and more aligned with the Integrists—but Selouteau knew the Elven rule had lasted for thousands of years. Should she really be questioning it?

More than that, she struggled with the idea of breaking protocol. Such actions had started the Necromancer's War and led to tens of thousands of Belissian deaths: Elves, Ez, Islanders and Swarmen had all died in the gruesome conflict, including her mother and Selouteau's own soldiers.

How was her father willing to follow such a path? And why had he involved her?

The sound of knocking brought her back to the present: she called to enter.

'Your mind is like a beacon,' said Perch, as he stalked through the door. 'So much conflict, and so much information ...'

'You will find yourself in a cell if you continue to peruse my mind uninvited. Especially when involved in sensitive discussions,' said Selouteau.

'Captain, you were broadcasting your thoughts to everyone with the mildest ability for Truthseeing. I came to stop you revealing something you shouldn't. Remember I told you that the Truthseeing isn't foolproof. There is a way to stop broadcasting your thoughts.'

'If that's true, then why do the Councils mandate debriefs with Truthseers?' asked Selouteau.

'Because most of the population don't know that Truthseers aren't infallible. Besides, the Truthseers themselves wouldn't divulge such a secret. It would destroy their credibility.' He walked around the table. 'It's not perfect, and a powerful Truthseer will be able to smash right through it, but the next time you feel your thoughts shouldn't be heard, concentrate on picturing an impenetrable wall and nothing else. Perhaps by the time a Truthseer realises what has happened, you'll be long gone.'

They made eye contact, and Selouteau felt as if Perch was much older than the youth he appeared to be. There was a cunning in his brown eyes that seemed to bore into the depths of her thoughts. She broke the eye contact and handed him the parchment map with the coordinates scrawled across it. 'Take these to Lieutenant Marillia at the helm. Have her plot course immediately, but tell her to remain as low as possible. I don't want to be seen where we are going.'

He nodded his understanding but didn't turn to leave. 'There might be more to your father than you know, but he loves you, Selouteau. He wouldn't ask you to do something against your own morals. You know that.'

CHAPTER FOUR

ON DECK, SELOUTEAU'S silver uniform was immaculate in the morning light. Her black boots were rooted in a wide stance, as she steadied herself against the swaying airship deck. She checked over the instrument stacks and the multitude of gauges built into the forward panel of the helm before her. The flicking arrows and steady pointers were all reading normal, and nodding to Lieutenant Marillia seated behind the helm, Selouteau ordered, 'Take us down.'

The Helmswoman acknowledged, her confident hands dancing over buttons, levers and control switches. Then, throttling back the main drives and placing two hands on the control column, she pushed forward. And their sleek, Elven airship dove from the sky.

Selouteau considered her ship's rakish silhouette. It was low and fast, with smooth lines and a long, pointed bow that flowed rearward into three interconnected hulls. The helm sat tightly within the wheelhouse at the vessel's rear, its small aft castle rising slightly above the main deck. Large, triangular sails, billowed in the morning breeze, the shimmering material gathering light from the twin suns to fuel three powerful crystal engines. She'd aptly named the airship the *Manoeuvre*; its unique design lent it unmatched speed and agility in preference over firepower.

As the bow dipped below the horizon, air whipped at Selouteau's uniform, and she gripped the back of Marillia's chair. The Helmswoman worked the controls, hauling several levers to stow the solar sails, and powered by unseen pulleys, the sails furled upwards, coiling within their protective sheaths along the lateen spars. The airship surged downwards, towards a canyon that looked like a gigantic scar across the land.

'The Rift?' asked Selouteau.

'Aye, Captain. You asked for a course that would mean fewer eyes on the *Manoeuvre*. Since no other airship has our speed and agility, we're able to navigate the Rift, and no one can follow. No one will see us in there.'

Selouteau stared at the back of the pilot's head for a moment, wondering if she'd lost her mind. The Elven Armada avoided the deep crevasse and jagged cliffs for a reason: their airships were faster and smoother at higher altitudes—and less likely to break upon the sharp rocks. But the more she thought about it, the more it made sense. The deserted canyon was perfect to remain unseen, and the *Manoeuvre's* agility meant they could move unhindered in the tight passages.

Selouteau eyed the great canyon that split the Belissian continent from tip to tip. As long as someone was brave enough to fly it, it was perfect. She nodded. 'Very good, Lieutenant Marillia. Proceed.'

Marillia steered the ship down towards the middle of the Rift's length. A sudden pocket of turbulence rocked the ship, and Selouteau heard a stumble from behind her. Wreadallanon, the onboard healer and younger brother of the late Ambassador Tendallanon, looked ungainly as he straightened and saluted her.

'Lieutenant Wread,' Selouteau greeted him, 'ensure all non-essential personnel, including yourself, are safely below decks. We don't want to lose anyone overboard as we move through these cliffs.'

He nodded and battled against the wind to disappear below deck. She watched him go as she gripped the back of Marillia's chair for balance. She worried about Wread's mental state since he'd learned about his brother's death. She knew he'd been particularly fond of his older brother, looking on him as a role model. And she knew it was only natural that the death would affect him deeply. It surprised her that the Truthseers had passed the Lieutenant for active duty; it felt too soon. But she had to maintain her confidence in Wread and give him the benefit of the doubt. He was a brilliant

Aquamancer, and if he was hiding anything that threatened the safety of himself or the crew, Perch would warn her. That's what the Truthseer was for.

Before Selouteau could think on it anymore, the airship plunged below ground level, streaking downwards between the cliffs.

Hauling back on the controls to level flight, Lieutenant Marillia tapped a power gauge in front of her, as the grey rocks closed in around the airship. 'We had full power when I retracted the solar sails, Captain, so we'll have enough energy to move down here for a handful of hours without direct light from the suns.'

'Define handful.'

Marillia turned to face the Captain, her flying goggles magnifying her eyes to buglike proportions. 'Three or so, depending how hard we push her.' She nodded as if acknowledging her own answer. 'More than enough to reach the Western County in the Rift's south and the open sunslight there.'

'Very good. She's all yours, Lieutenant.'

'With pleasure,' said Marillia, smiling with genuine delight.

Pilots, Selouteau rolled her eyes, *they're all the same.*

Lieutenant Marillia wove the *Manoeuvre* through the canyon, her hands a constant blur. Forever adjusting and readjusting the control surfaces, she rolled the sleek airship from left to right, as they sped through the tight bends with reckless abandon.

Built for nimbleness, the *Manoeuvre* was designed to keep crew activities below deck, so the airship could buck and weave through the skies—or canyons—without fear of losing anyone overboard. Therefore, the designers had constructed the *Manoeuvre* without deck railings, which added a significant speed advantage over airships of similar size.

And it shows, thought Selouteau with pride, as she leaned into another sharp turn.

Her mind drifted to thoughts of the possibility of another Belissian war and what it would mean. She found her mind drifting to Perch and why the Truthseer would have told her about the Truthseeing not being foolproof. *Could it be possible?*

The morning passed quickly. Every so often, Selouteau checked to see if Marillia showed any signs of fatigue, but the pilot was relentless. And, just as she had promised, after two hours within the crevasse, they suddenly left the confines of the Rift and hurtled into open air.

In one beautiful moment, the gorge opened, and the *Manoeuvre* streaked from the darkness into the shining daylight above the deep, lush valley of the Western County. The golden sails unfurled with a flourish and snapped loudly as they billowed to capacity. Glittering in the suns' rays, the ship begun to hum, as solar energy was collected by the sails and distributed between the engines.

Surrounded by steep cliffs in every direction but south, the leagues-wide valley shone with greens of the deepest hues. Selouteau took in the expanse with awe. The forest's impenetrable canopies looked like an ocean, rolling in endless waves. But here and there, the foliage gave way to the towering trunks of the bizarre mushroom trees, their colossal heights looming above the forest below.

Marillia guided them closer to one of the mushroom trees. They were many times larger than the *Manoeuvre,* and Selouteau eyed the rubbery surface as they traced a smooth arc around it before dropping below its rim to expose the brown gills of the underside. A flock of feasting birds took flight from their perches, scattering in the airship's wake as the pilot, then turned them to an easterly heading.

Selouteau loved that her position as captain of a vessel took her all over the Belissian countryside but hated having no time to enjoy it, or take stock of Belissia's natural beauty on mission. There was just never enough time.

'They don't grow like this in our city of Darkwood, do they?' said Marillia, as she examined the mushroom trees with appreciation.

Selouteau shook her head in reply. Darkwood was Selouteau's least favourite of the Elven cities. Cold, damp, dark and littered with thousands of mushrooms that grew as tall as an Elf. It remained the only completely underground Elven city, and though it was nearly overrun with mushroom trees, they were hundreds of times smaller than the ones they now circled. 'I've been told the sunslight, calm winds and fertile soil here nourish them. No words could be more incorrect to describe Darkwood.'

Marillia chuckled, then examined a portion of a Belissian map on a small pedestal to the right of her instrument panel. 'The coordinates put Prince Ezell's position somewhere over there.' She pointed portside, off the bow. 'Do we know what we're looking for?'

Selouteau regarded the area Marillia indicated. 'Not exactly. However, Grand Admiral Synnathril mentioned the Prince hiding in a set of caves. His directions were as detailed as 'near the valley's rim' at the coordinates I supplied you.'

The Lieutenant nodded her understanding, and Selouteau felt herself wondering from where her father got his information. The fact that he'd made this move outside the Councils hinted that he had informants reporting directly to him. Selouteau knew her father was regularly well informed—due to his position as Grand Admiral—but the idea that her father had spies reporting directly to him seemed … dirty.

Marillia cut through her thoughts. 'Captain, shall I point her in that direction?'

'Yes, Lieutenant, thank you. Let's find a spot to put down.'

They continued their steady descent toward the eastern rim of the valley, banking around the trunks of the mushroom trees that poked through the foliage here and there. There was little place to land in the dense forest, but with skill, Marillia picked a landing zone as close to the cliffs as possible. Sliding the ship through a gap in the canopies, she landed them in a shadowed glade, bordered by a burbling stream, its glassy water tracking lazily over rounded boulders.

Selouteau eyed the surrounds for movement. Seeing nothing, she pulled a handheld Globcomm from her uniform, checked the settings remained on crew frequency and thumbed the activation switch. 'Commander Lieffendroon, Lieutenant Wread and Ensign Perch, report to the helm.'

Filing onto the deck, the required crew grouped around the wheelhouse at the stern of the vessel. She cut straight to the point.

'We are here in the Western County looking for Ezell, Prince of the Ez. He has moved into self-imposed exile based on the King of the Ez's decision to enter negotiations with the Humans and has since gone into hiding in these cliffs. Specifically, we are looking for a cave system.' She indicated the cliffs in question, their looming shape still visible despite the thick canopy above them. 'Ensign Perch and Lieutenant Wread, you'll come with me.' Her gaze shifted to her tall, gallant second-in-command: 'Commander Lieffendroon, the ship is yours.'

'Do you have any recommendations, Captain?' asked the Commander, inclining his sharp-featured face.

'Pull back to a respectable distance and monitor the airways. You might find a suitable tether beneath one of those mushroom trees where you won't be seen from any passing traffic above. Make sure our journey here remains unnoticed and listen for any communication from the Grand Admiral. Notify me via Globcomm if he makes contact. Any further questions?'

When no one spoke, she dismissed him and waved Perch and Wread to her side. Together, the three of them slipped over the railless deck to the glade, only a yard below the hovering airship.

Their boots sank into the soft ground, and striding to a safe distance from the ship, they watched as the *Manoeuvre's* engines surged with power, and waves of air rolled across the grass. With a growing whine, the sleek warship rose from the earth, bobbing slightly as it swung to face the west. Then, blasting its hot exhaust, it slid through the canopy and powered away.

'You know, I never grow tired of that ship. It is truly magnificent,' said Perch, gazing in awe.

'Thank you, Ensign. Now, listen, I want you to hide your Truthseeing from the Ez. Use it to gauge reactions and seek the Truth, but nothing extravagant. I'm unsure how this will pan out, and we need to keep a few tricks in reserve.'

'And me?'

Selouteau studied Wread.

'With all due respect, Captain, I'm a healer, not a mindless Juian. I know why you've brought me along.'

'For all you know, Juians might be incredibly intelligent creatures,' interjected Perch.

Wread paused to regard the Truthseer, an expression of annoyance marring his features. He turned back to Selouteau, his dark brown eyes showing suspicion. 'You're keeping an eye on me, aren't you, Captain?'

Selouteau answered easily, her career as an officer lending her grace under pressure. 'That's not entirely true, Lieutenant. You're a gifted Aquamancer, and I think you could use some time in the field. It will give you a distraction from your loss. The fact that I want to keep an eye on you stems from a concern for all my crew.'

Wread nodded, though Selouteau could tell he was unimpressed. Not that it mattered. Her job was to lead the crew, not be friends with them. It was a lesson she'd learned the hard way during the Necromancer's War. Losing her mother was one thing, but receiving a promotion over her dead soldiers was something else. Selouteau broke away from the thought and turned to the Truthseer. 'Perch, you take the lead. I'll bring up the rear.'

They crossed the burbling stream, bounding with Elven grace from boulder to boulder before moving into the thick forest. They then started the steady climb towards the rock formations above. Weaving between rough trunks and around dense thickets, they ascended in silence.

Again, Selouteau wondered why her father had sent her on this mission. He knew her strengths lay in tactics and war, not politics or diplomacy. The names of several skilled negotiators came to mind, far better equipped to persuade the Prince of the Ez. Since the outcome of her mission could influence the threat of war, why not use an officer with greater experience? Other than the fact that as his daughter, he could trust her, Selouteau didn't think the choice to send her made any sense.

The smell of moist undergrowth reached Selouteau as she considered her knowledge of Belissia's history: the Lesser Races had been trying to break away from Elven rule for centuries, but each attempt had been quelled by the Elven Councils. It was logical for the King of the Ez to think the Humans could help them achieve independence. But it sickened her to think he was turning to a race they knew nothing about. She wished the Lesser Races would give the Integrists a little more time to push out the Traditionalist incumbents.

As they moved through a particularly dense patch of undergrowth, Selouteau wondered why the Councils refused to acknowledge the possibility of another war, despite the obvious signs. Exclusive trade deals, the hiking of tariffs and now the Ez cutting ties with the Elves: the Humans had invaded Belissia, just not in the way that the Elves had first thought.

Sounds drifted through the undergrowth, obscured by the densely packed foliage. Her long

Elven ears twitched to catch the guttural grunts, and she caught the heady whiff of carrion.

'Ugh, sounds like a pack of Juians,' said Perch. 'Did you know they look like a crazy, sharp-toothed monkey crossed with a hairy ant? Nasty little creatures.'

Wread tensed. 'I know what they look like, Ensign. But there's no need to be afraid, they're just little beasts. Not very intelligent.'

'I've heard they have a horrible bite,' said Perch. 'You know, it's always intrigued me how the Councils classify the Lesser Races. For example, what criteria do they use to group non-Elven Belissians?'

'The Juians aren't classified in the Lesser Races,' said Wread.

'Yes, because the Councils believe the Juians aren't smart enough to have them differentiated from beasts,' Perch responded. 'But at what point does the Councils consider them smart enough? When do they decide vicious creatures like the Juians and those big, black panthers the Ez ride are smart enough to be catalogued in the Lesser Races with the Ez, Swarmen and Islanders?' He ticked them off on his fingers.

A male voice speaking in the native Ez language interrupted from the undergrowth: 'You Elves are all the same. Arrogant and small minded.'

Selouteau whipped her sword out. Her feet slid into a wide stance, and she signalled the Elves to form a defensive triangle at her back. There they rotated slowly, eyes raking the surrounding forest.

Brushing foliage aside, a black panther—as tall as the Elves—padded menacingly into the small clearing. Across its broad back sat a figure in scarlet and black armour, two loaded crossbows held tightly in his gloved hands. The sharp quarrel tips were levelled at Selouteau's chest. And before she could open her mouth to speak, one fired with a loud twang.

CHAPTER FIVE

THE QUARREL WHIZZED past Selouteau's face—close enough to ruffle her hair—and buried itself in a tree behind her with a loud thud. A warning shot. The panther rider chuckled, his identity hidden behind a black helm, emblazoned with a scarlet hand. He spoke with a typical Southern Ez accent that sounded like a drawl to her Elven ears; the Ez language was considered a shorthand version of the Elven tongue.

'Now, what brings three Elves to the Western County? This isn't the safest place to be lurking; perhaps even more so when hearing that we'll be at war with your race soon.'

Selouteau watched as the rider scanned the trees around them before she spoke in his language: 'We're here to find Prince Ezell of the Ez. I'm hoping you could take us to him.'

'What makes you think I know where he is?'

'Your amour is that of an Ez Royal Guard,' said Selouteau.

'And you're a long way from the Ez capital of Ezguard. Perhaps you are on a secret mission to protect the Prince in Exile?' Perch chimed in.

Selouteau, though unable to see the rider's eyes, felt the weight of his gaze. He lifted the crossbows and removed the remaining bolt, holstering both weapons. 'It's true there's a division among the Ez.'

'To be this deep in the Western County, you must be one of the Prince's men. Please, we need an audience,' said Selouteau, motioning for Perch and Wread to lower their weapons.

The rider laughed. 'This is only the edge of the Western County, lady Elf! You'll find the beasts far more vicious further in.'

Growling deep in its throat, the panther accentuated the rider's comment by baring its teeth.

'That's quite intimidating,' said Perch with a nervous laugh, though Selouteau could tell the Truthseer was feigning.

'Only if you don't know how to talk to them,' said the guard, as he patted the large cat's shoulder blades. 'Come, I will take you to the Prince. He thought the Elves might be sending a negotiator.'

He pointed them up the rising terrain and tugged at the reins of the great panther he was riding. The creature remained still, fixing each Elf with its iridescent green eyes and growling. Again, the rider tugged, and with a roll of its great head, the panther obeyed.

Taking point, the Ez rider and his mount set a meandering pace upwards.

Once sure that they were out of earshot, Selouteau leaned into Perch and whispered in Elven: 'Did you know he was there?'

'Yes.'

'Then why didn't you say something?' said Selouteau.

Perch cocked an eyebrow. 'You told me to pretend I wasn't a Truthseer.'

'Not to the exclusion of warning me of a threat.'

'Captain, he's not a threat. Look at him,' said Perch.

She took a moment to watch the smooth, unhurried movements and relaxed pace of the Ez's mount. Perch was right. Both rider and panther moved with an air of bored familiarity that made Selouteau think the guard felt at home in the dense undergrowth of the Western County.

'And what is your name, young Ez?' said Selouteau, again speaking in the Ez language.

'I am Wilhelm Torla, second son of Count Solvaard Torla, who is the Lord of Gavidgeon and the Western County.'

Selouteau introduced herself and her companions before continuing the small talk. 'You're from Gavidgeon? I thought you looked at home here.'

'Yes. Though, I prefer the forests farther to the south.' Wilhelm pointed one red-and-black gauntlet south along the escarpment now visible as they climbed out of the forests.

'I've always wanted to see the Ez's fortress city of Gavidgeon,' said Perch.

'I can't see how that will ever happen. The Elves haven't set foot in Gavidgeon since the Night of the Lost. My father won't allow it. And even if the tensions between our races settle, I can't see my father's opinion changing any time soon,' said Wilhelm.

Selouteau felt the wounds of their races' history surfacing: the Elves had assassinated the previous Lord of the Western County, and though that was common knowledge, no one outside of the Councils knew why—other than the usual 'it was for their own safety'.

They passed from dense foliage to the sparse, rocky outcrops at the base of the cliffs in silence. Above them, the towering escarpment marked the edge of the Rift, and behind them was the entire Western County, bordered by the valley's sharp walls.

In front, the rider continued without stopping for the view, his mount pacing between cart-sized boulders with feline grace. Selouteau followed until they slipped beneath a deeply shadowed overhang where it took a moment for her eyes to adjust. When they did adjust, she saw several Ez Royal Guards standing watch, their spears held before them.

Beyond the guards, Selouteau could see a bustling scene. Figures covered in the eye-catching armour of the Ez Royal Guard travelled back and forth, moving crates, saddles and weapons. The Ez were much smaller and slighter than the Elves, and even with their armour on, Selouteau thought they looked unnaturally small.

On her right lazed a mass of panthers, the exact number impossible to count as they cuddled together, but judging by the size of their paws, Selouteau wagered they were equal in size to Wilhelm's—if not larger.

On her left, an untidy stack of supplies was being efficiently dismantled and carried deep within the cave. An officer, evident by the crimson cape falling from his broad shoulders and the slate board he held, called out quiet orders. Under his direction, marching Ez passed through little pools of light spilling from the oil lanterns that were hung along the cave's wall. They continued deeper into the cave and disappeared within a tunnel at the rear.

'There must be a hundred Ez here,' Selouteau muttered in Elven. 'I didn't think the Prince in Exile would possess that much of a following.'

'Actually, there are ninety-eight soldiers here,' Perch whispered. 'Truthseeing makes it easy to count their minds.'

Wilhelm swung down from his mount, and as the Ez's armoured boots crashed against the stone, Selouteau looked down at the Royal Guard; he was far shorter than she had realised.

'Tell me, Wilhelm, are all Ez as short as you?' said Perch, not even trying to stifle his grin.

An approaching Ez—the officer with the red cape—laughed loudly and clapped the much smaller Wilhelm on the armour of his shoulder. He spoke in

Ez: 'No, not all Ez are as short as Wilhelm, though I can tell you none are as tall as yourselves.' He turned his green eyes up to the towering Elves, each standing a full head and shoulders above him. 'My name is Edric, Captain of the Royal Guard.'

Selouteau noted the controlled intonation in his speech, the kind that was trained into the Ez nobility. It gave them an almost regal air when speaking the language which was often described as bastardised Elven.

Wilhelm removed his helm, revealing a boyish, unbearded face and piercing blue eyes. He was much younger than Selouteau would have thought—barely older than a boy. His skin was the colour of most Ez: a caramel brown, as if they spent their life under the twin suns. 'I caught them on patrol, discussing their Lesser Race catalogues.'

'Charming,' said Edric. Lines creased the older Ez's forehead, and he scratched his shortly cropped hair. 'I gather you're here to see the Prince?'

'Immediately,' said Selouteau.

'He said you'd be coming, though you'll have to leave your weapons out here. I'm sure you're aware the situation in Belissia is about to get very ugly, and I'd hate for it to start here,' said Edric.

'And their sorcery?' said Wilhelm, his accent hanging onto each syllable.

'If we could take that, we would have done it already,' said Edric. 'You seem well acquainted, young Wilhelm; you can take them to the Prince. I'll have Zethish looked after.'

'Of course, Captain.' Wilhelm clanked a fist to his heart in a quick salute and tucking his helmet under his arm, he led them deeper into the bowl-shaped cave to a table beside an officer calling orders. 'Here, your weapons will be safe with the First Lieutenant.'

Selouteau motioned for Perch and Wread to disarm. She too reached for the sword that had been given to her by her father on receipt of her first command; so much had changed since then. She rested the slim blade atop the pile, and before entering the tunnel, she looked at the bustling scene once more. Selouteau noted that Wilhelm's panther watched her every move with intelligent eyes. She made eye contact with the beast, and wondered what that meant before following the short Ez solider into the tunnel beyond.

The passage continued much further than Selouteau would have thought, the little pools of yellow light stretching into the underground distance for as far as she could see. Wilhelm led them roughly fifteen paces into the tunnel, before turning left through a carved doorway that opened into a small cave-like room.

Ezell, Crown Prince of the Ez, heir to Ezguard and now Prince in Exile, stooped over a makeshift table. Selouteau bowed deeply, again noting the physical differences between their two races. Where the Elves were tall and athletic, the Ez were petite and slight of build. Where the Elves were black or blond of hair with brown eyes, the Ez had eyes of blue or green and hair of brown or shades of red. And where the Elves were pale and unblemished of skin, the Ez were caramel skinned—mottled with freckles and discolourations.

But strangely, for the race of Ez, Ezell was an anomaly.

He was taller than most and broader as well, and while shorter than an Elf, he cut a dashing figure with strong shoulders and a muscular build visible beneath his green tunic. And although Selouteau knew the Ez Prince was yet to see his eighteenth birthday, intelligence shone within his young blue eyes. When he looked at Selouteau, a smile pulled at his lips. Swishing his wavy blond hair and adjusting the sword dangling loosely from his belt, he moved around the table, arms held wide. 'I said the Elves would send a negotiator.'

Selouteau smiled politely. 'Your Royal Highness.'

He snorted. 'Hardly. Being in exile removes most of my liberties. Please, call me Prince Ezell.' He bowed, though not as low as Selouteau. 'I see you've already met my cousin, Wilhelm Torla.'

Selouteau nodded and introduced herself. 'I am Captain Selouteau of the Elven Armada, and these are Elves of my crew: Lieutenant Wreadallanon and Ensign Perch. We have come to discuss the Human threat.'

Ezell took the measure of each Elf as Selouteau introduced them. He indicated a set of low chairs pushed into the far corner of the room. 'Please, if we're turning to business, we'd best be comfortable, or as close to it as possible. I would normally offer you a hot tea, but …' he shrugged at his meagre surroundings, 'we'll have to make do for now.'

Selouteau sat on one of the hard chairs, and Prince Ezell seated himself across from her, strong legs spread wide as he leaned forward and spoke first: 'It's been some time since our races have participated in an open, honest negotiation.'

'The Elves have maintained open communication with the Ez for centuries,' said Selouteau.

'Fifty years ago—before my own birth—Elven forces swarmed two Ez cities in the middle of the night. They killed hundreds of Ez, many whose bodies were never recovered. And we were never given an explanation. How is that healthy communication?'

'It was necessary for the safety of all Ez,' said Selouteau, though in Truth she wished she knew why the event had occurred.

'Yes, let's talk about that. Many Ez simply think the Elves are mass murderers. They *want* to go to war with you. But I believe there is more to it. Explain why the Elves almost brought us to the brink of war for "our safety".' He too spoke his language with the same regal control as the captain of the guard.

Selouteau cursed her father. He said this conversation would be easy. 'First, I'd like to state that I was not party to the operations that night; I am deeply sorrowed by the loss of your people. Second, as I understand it, the Elven Councils became aware of a threat within the Ez population that would have proven fatal if left uncontrolled. They acted to remove the threat, much like the removal of a swamp raptor's poison. I'm sure your father would have more details than I.'

'My father refuses to speak about it. The Ez are not as long lived as the Elves, Captain Selouteau. He was a boy of nine in those years. Having lived through the Night of the Lost and the Necromancer's War, he hates the Elves,' said Prince Ezell.

'The Necromancer's War was brought about by a murderer who made war to prove a point,' said Selouteau. 'Vylok didn't stand for the values of the Elven population.'

'Yes, but the curfews and mandatory camps imposed by the Elves during that war removed liberties and resulted in tens of thousands of deaths. You cannot honestly say my people were safe in those camps, Captain.'

'They died because they were killed by the Necromancer. Elves too died in their defence, might I add,' said Selouteau.

'They were fenced in like animals. Herded for their own protection and then murdered by one of your own.'

Selouteau took a moment to centre her thoughts. She could feel her anger rising. She'd lost her entire first command to the Necromancer's attack on the camp she was defending. She'd been promoted for her actions there. The Elven Armada thought her courageous, but she felt the entire operation and the loss of life could be nothing other than a failure.

The Prince continued. 'You can't be surprised that my father is looking to free himself from your reign.'

Selouteau willed her memories to silence. Now wasn't the time, especially because she knew the Prince spoke the Truth. And she too hated the oppressive nature of the Traditionalist Elven Councils. 'I am truly sorry, Prince Ezell. The Integrist Elves are trying to move away from such autocratic control, and they are gaining support. The fact that the Councils sent me here proves they're trying.' She let the lie fall from her tongue.

The barest movement caught her eye, as Wilhelm's hand tightened on the hilt of his sword. The Prince noted his cousin's subtle motion before leaning forwards, rubbing at the smattering of blond stubble on his chin. 'Why did you come here today? What is it that you want?'

'We are here to discuss the possibility of a new future. We think the Humans are preparing for a war on Belissia and may be recruiting the Ez to their cause.'

'And you want to round us up again? Stop us from protecting ourselves?' said the Prince, his lips set in a firm line.

Selouteau had no doubt that some of the Traditionalists would want to do exactly that. But she masked her emotions as best she could, refusing to let the Prince know he'd struck a nerve.

When she didn't reply, he said: 'They're here on a religious crusade, Captain. Searching for artefacts demanded by their Divine-King. What makes you think they're here for war?'

Selouteau gathered her thoughts. She would rather be on the battlefield than conducting this kind of political manoeuvring. She hated that she was in this position: stuck between the Councils' expectations and what she felt was right. The thought caused her mind to falter. If the Councils discovered what she was doing—what her father had asked her to do—her military career would be over. There was no doubt about it. Everything she'd worked for, years of achievements to prove herself worthy of her parents' titles would be for naught.

She considered the Prince in Exile and found she felt connected to him, as if their paths were complementary. He was a Prince in self-imposed exile. The passion in his voice showed that he cared about his people and would lose everything to protect them. Selouteau realised they were more alike than she cared to imagine. Because if the Councils ever discovered what she was about to say, she would lose everything.

'A little over six weeks ago,' Selouteau began, 'the Humans arrived on Belissian soil and were reported by an airship patrol, before the ship and the crew disappeared. Without proof that the Humans were responsible for the disappearance, the Councils sent an Ambassador, who also vanished. Until ...' She detailed her attack on Gusting and conveniently left out Perch's Truthseeing. She explained how she and Perch had escaped with the Ambassador, who unfortunately died shortly after as a result of his wounds at the hands of the Humans. She noticed Wread stiffen beside her at the mention of his brother's name and looked long enough to also see Perch's steady gaze, but she continued regardless.

She told of the thousands of Human troops they'd seen make landfall and outlined the secret trade agreement the Southern Islanders had signed. She pointed to how such price hikes would impact all Belissian trade and likely widen the rift within the Islander people.

'The Islanders have always been at each other's throats,' interjected the Prince, 'but they remain our largest trading ally—'

'They are everybody's largest trading ally,' said Selouteau. 'The Islanders are the wellspring for all trade. They are Belissia's trade. Can you see what this points to?'

Ezell chewed the inside of his lip. 'I can see why you think the agreement would destabilise our markets. Yet, if the Humans' troops have landed in such great number, why is this the first we've heard of it?'

'I wager the Elven Councils kept it from your King, concerned the Ez would see it as an opportunity.'

'Well, the Councils would be correct if that was true … So do you think that the Humans are trying to starve Belissia to sabotage the Elves?'

'I'm not sure, but an unfed opponent is easily defeated,' said Selouteau.

Ezell nodded, his young face screwed up in thought. 'Let's say I believe the Humans are tempting my people into their war with the Elves, and that I disagree with overthrowing the Elven reign so strongly that I abandoned my father in an effort to stall the negotiations … What would you have me do? If the Humans and the Elves do go to war, there is nothing my people can do to stop either side. We'll be pawns and cannon fodder.'

'Is there a way the Elven Councils could meet with your King? We hope to present our case before he sides with the Humans.'

The Prince grimaced. 'My father is due to meet with Governor Thawn tomorrow. It might be impossible to see him before then.'

Selouteau swore internally. She hadn't realised the Ez King would move that fast. 'Wait, who is Governor Thawn?'

'Governor Thawn is the instrument of their God's divine intention. He enacts the Divine-King's religious crusade and oversees the search for their artefacts here on Belissia. Thawn commands all military and civilian decisions.'

Was this more information the Councils knew and hadn't passed along? Selouteau smothered her reaction and moved the topic back to the Ez King: 'You said the meeting is tomorrow?'

'Yes. I went into exile hoping it would slow the proceedings and make my father rethink his decision. Unfortunately, the soldiers inform me it remains on track. They are due to sign an agreement tomorrow.'

'Do you know the terms of the agreement?'

He shook his head, before suddenly his eyes lit up. 'What if we were there?' The Prince pointed at Selouteau. 'What if we captured the Governor and renegotiated the Humans' departure from Belissia? We could stop my people from joining the Humans, and you could stop your war before it begins.'

Selouteau watched as the Prince stood to consider the idea, his hand rubbing at the patchy stubble on his chin. He turned to regard her once more, his blue eyes dancing. 'If you want to prove the Elves are serious about changing their ways, then you should share the risk. You should be there with me.'

CHAPTER SIX

‘HE WANTS TO *what*?’ said Syn. And even through the Globcomm, Selouteau could hear the stress in her father's voice.

‘He wants to capture the Governor and renegotiate the terms of the Ez treaty so the Humans leave Belissia,’ Selouteau repeated.

She watched the stormy innards of the Globcomm whip and lash with her father's clipped syllables: ‘I had such high hopes for Ezell as the next King of the Ez, but he's acting like a child. He is a child. If we are party to that attack, we could provoke the Humans into war.’

‘And if the Humans are preparing for war anyway, this might be our only chance,’ said Selouteau. ‘We could stop them before they're ready. Before they can do any more damage.’

‘All right, you have my permission. But there are to be no casualties, Selouteau. Non-lethal force only. This operation is still unsanctioned by the

Councils, and if the Humans have even the slightest reason to retaliate …' He left the idea hanging in the air between them.

'I understand,' said Selouteau.

'Selouteau, at the first sign of trouble, I want you to abort, even if the Prince's life is in danger.'

'Dad, Prince Ezell asked for our assistance. We are trying to mend ties with the Ez, not break them. Leaving their Prince in danger if we encounter resistance will not help this process. Our success with Prince Ezell could be a real win for the Integrists.'

'Unfortunately, the Prince does not represent the Ez majority, Selouteau. Prince Ezell said that much himself. It seems the Ez King has made his decision, even if the Prince does not support it. *Our* decision is about mitigating the damage of the Humans' arrival. You must look to the bigger picture, Selouteau. The Ez Prince can be dealt with, after the present situation.'

Selouteau nodded, though she didn't agree. She wanted to help the Prince, because it seemed their best chance at averting a much larger war, not to mention a chance to prove the Integrists' intentions. But she knew her rank. 'Understood, Grand Admiral.'

Selouteau pushed herself away from the table and strode out of her quarters onto the deck of the *Manoeuvre*. They floated high above the Western County, many hours' flight from home and less than an hours' flight from the Ez capital—Ezguard. Halfway between the northern and southern tips of Belissia, they were effectively in the middle of nowhere.

Overhead, the sky was awash with pinks, purples and bright oranges from the setting suns now outlined beyond the Border Ranges to the west of the Rift. Floating at this altitude meant that Selouteau could communicate via Globcomm without interruption or interference from the surrounding landscape. Examining the beautiful setting of the suns, Selouteau motioned the pilot, Marillia, to lower the airship so she could return to Ezell's caves. She'd excused herself from the Prince in Exile to discuss things with her father, the commanding officer.

Perch paced silently to stand beside her, and together they watched the twin suns disappear over the Border Ranges. Beneath their feet, the airship lowered to the darkening forests.

'Do you believe what you said earlier, Captain?' said Perch. 'About us removing the dangerous Ez so they couldn't do any harm, and that it was for the safety of all Ez.'

'Why wouldn't I?'

'Because our Councils don't exactly have the cleanest slate when it comes to the Truth,' said Perch.

'What are you insinuating, Ensign?'

'What if I told you that the Councils were cleaning up a mess that they created, and the Ez were simply cannonfodder? And that the Necromancer discovered the Councils' games and started a war to overthrow them ... What if the Necromancer wanted to protect Belissia from the Elven Councils?'

She laughed. 'That's very conspiratorial of you, young Ensign. Even if it were true, neither the Necromancer or the Councils did a very good job of protecting Belissia. The Prince made that clear today.'

'Indeed,' Perch turned to her, the setting suns' still-bright colours illuminating his blond hair. 'Do you believe in the Purge, Captain? We've prepared for its return for one thousand nine hundred and sixty-seven years, and yet, not once in that time have there been any sightings or evidence to prove the Purge exists.'

'But there are those who remember the Purge War,' said Selouteau.

'Only King Eltavar and Neberadar the Grand Librarian—the two highest-ranking Elves—are old enough to recall any details. Even the Acolytes of the Great Library have failed to find any scriptures on the Purge's existence, let alone an all-encompassing war that we had to be rescued from. The King and the Grand Librarian are the biggest stalwarts for Traditionalism and the push for Purge preparation. It surely is a great story to keep the Elves in line: training for a war that may never have happened and may never come.'

'The last time somebody questioned the Councils like that, the Necromancer dragged us into a war,' said Selouteau. She slipped from the airship's deck to the soft grass, billowing below the hovering airship.

She heard Perch drop to the glade behind her and mutter, 'Vylok had his reasons.'

Without a chance to consider the Truthseer's words, Selouteau bowed to Prince Ezell, who sat regally atop a panther, its black nose raised into the hot breeze of the Manoeuvre's exhaust. Two Royal Guards flanked him—their black helms splattered with a painted red hand. Selouteau nodded towards the Guard she knew as Wilhelm, as the Prince and his Ez watched the receding airship.

'You know, nothing would bridge the equality gap between the Elves and the other races more than sharing your airships,' said Prince Ezell, his blue eyes tracking the shrinking glow of her airship's engine wash.

'That is something I cannot promise. You and I both know the Elven Councils would never agree to that; at least not until the Integrists have more Council seats,' said Selouteau.

'With airships, the Elves are the only Belissians who have the ability to travel long distances quickly and with little effort. Think how positively that would affect all Belissian trade.'

'I'm sorry, Prince Ezell,' said Selouteau, 'that is something I cannot give you. Not yet, at least.'

'We must arrange another form of payment then,' said Prince Ezell. He beckoned and spurred his mount up the darkening hills, his Royal Guards flanking.

'Payment?' said Selouteau.

'Yes, for providing the opportunity to end this war before it begins.'

'Our assistance in the capture of Governor Thawn is our payment,' said Selouteau.

'Come now, I'm providing you with an opportunity to prevent thousands more needless deaths. Without me, you'd be unaware of Thawn's location, and I know you want him as badly as I do. I think the Elves can offer something better.'

'You obviously have something in mind,' said Selouteau.

'Perhaps you can help us with our border control. The Swarmen are becoming increasingly threatening. I had planned to police them with our soldiers, but your Elven assistance would go a long way,' said Prince Ezell.

Selouteau recalled what she knew of the amphibious aquatic creatures that lived in the Coastal Swamps to the east of the Ez's land. The Swarmen had no formal government and preferred to live in a smattering of feudal tribes and often turned to harassing Islander and Ez civilians, seeing them as easier targets than opposing tribal factions.

'The Swarmen raid our eastern lands, harassing farmers and villagers. Your help to shore up our borders would guarantee the safety of those farmers, and I'm sure feelings towards the Elves would improve.'

Selouteau nodded. It would look good for the Integrists. 'You play this political game well, Prince Ezell.'

'I was brought up in the courts of Ezguard, studying politics as often as swordplay and history. But the Ez nobles had to learn their behaviour from somewhere,' said the Prince.

'Indeed.'

'He's good,' said Perch, nodding his approval towards the Prince. 'He's very good.'

Passing into the deep shadows beneath the overhang of the Prince's hideout, Selouteau found the bustling soldiers from earlier had gone, leaving the bowl-like cave feeling cold and empty. Only five guards stood on duty, three at the cave's entrance and two at the tunnel's mouth. She eyed the guards as their black and scarlet armour melded easily with the shadows around them.

'This is an impressive cave system,' said Selouteau. 'An easily defensible position that retreats into a bottleneck.'

Ezell nodded as he dismounted, handing his reins to the Royal Guard on his right. Wilhelm followed suit, and they followed the Prince deeper down the tunnel, passing small openings on the left and right that showed cramped chambers and more hallways beyond.

Selouteau noticed an unnatural perfection in the straightness of the tunnel, as well as the way that the side corridors were spaced at regular intervals—and at perfect right angles. She ran her eyes over what looked like tooling marks in the ceiling and walls and noted they passed small bottlenecks every four doorways.

'These caves were built by the Ez.' The words came out more as statement than question.

'Yes, Captain,' said Prince Ezell. 'Though designed to look natural, they were built shortly before the last Belissian war as a refuge and safe house for some of the Ez nobles. Constructed underground for safety, they were consistently stocked with all necessary supplies.'

'We're a fair distance from Ezguard. Travelling across the open Blue Plains between here and your capital wouldn't be the safest option during war,' said Selouteau.

'Luckily, they thought of that, too,' said Ezell. He turned left, leading them into the same chamber as earlier that morning. Rifling through the maps stacked neatly on one corner of the table, he set one in the centre with a sudden 'Aha.' Securing the map's corners with brass paperweights, he revealed a scrawled plan of the cave's myriad passages and chambers.

Selouteau looked at the design with genuine surprise. The passages led far deeper than she would have thought.

'Does that stretch all the way to Ezguard?' Perch pointed to a long, straight tunnel ending in an arrow labelled Ezguard.

The Prince nodded.

'Does the King know you are here?' asked Selouteau.

'Yes, my father knows about the tunnels, but being busy with the Humans, I don't think he'll be coming after us any time soon.' He paused before pointing to several key locations on the map. 'We've placed sentries at the Ezguard entrances and rigged a small collapse in case they are swamped or followed. Without the direct route from Ezguard, these tunnels are very difficult to find at the edge of the Rift.'

'So we discovered,' said Selouteau.

'Our plans were to take stock counts of the refuge stores here, which you saw us doing earlier. With those counts, we know how long we'll survive without needing to leave. I thought we could use these caves as our home for now … To be honest, I'd not considered exile before the Humans began negotiations with my father. It's not something I've planned terribly well.'

'I doubt exile is something anyone plans, but you seem to be coping well enough. Prince Ezell, I have to be frank: you have more followers here than I would have expected, especially as you are so young.'

'Some are here out of loyalty to myself, but others truly believe the Humans are a threat. Speaking with complete candour, I was not expecting this many.'

'How did you contact them all?' Perch interrupted suddenly, his brown eyes searching the young Prince's face. 'How did you know who to trust and who wouldn't reveal your secret to the King?'

'I'm a Prince ... I have my ways.'

The Truthseer frowned in thought, and Selouteau knew him well enough to know he was onto something, but her thoughts were interrupted as the young Ez, Wilhelm, walked up to the table and said: 'Should we discuss the plan for tomorrow's attack?'

'Of course,' said Ezell.

Selouteau critiqued and questioned as Ezell detailed his plan. And in the back of her mind, she considered the likely outcomes in light of her father's requests; the mission must be successful, and no lives were to be lost.

If the Governor were to escape without signing a renegotiation, then the chances were high he would resort to war. And, if any Humans were killed in the operation, they would have firm grounds for an attack. Again, Selouteau worried about the lack of Council approval. She felt as if the very future of Belissia depended on tomorrow's outcome.

As the Prince rounded up his conclusion, Selouteau nodded. 'All things considered, the plan should go as expected. Unless there is something you've missed.'

'My soldiers are still within Ezguard's citadel and provide reports every four hours. If there is something we've missed, we'll know about it before we move.'

Footsteps sounded behind them as Lieutenant Wread strode through the opening into the room, his silvery officer's uniform was covered in patches of dark blood across his forearms and chest.

'Where have you been?' Perch asked, eyeing the blood.

Wread turned his dark eyes on the Truthseer. 'Not that it's any of your business, Ensign, and nor do you have the rank to question me as such, but Captain Selouteau asked me to help Prince Ezell with his injured men.'

'Thank you for allowing Lieutenant Wread-allanon to help here, Captain. We truly appreciate his healing abilities.' Ezell bowed his head to Selouteau.

'Please take it as a token of sincerity and to show that the Integrists are gaining power.'

Wread helped himself to a tumbler of water from a table nearby. 'How did you say these injuries happened?'

'Our departure from Ezguard didn't go completely unnoticed; we ran into some trouble. It complicates things when you're fighting an opponent you don't want to hurt, and civil war is something I won't ever condone.'

'But you went into exile for conflicting views with your King?' said Selouteau.

Ezell squared his shoulders. 'Exile and civil war aren't the same thing. My views are different to my father's, but that doesn't mean I'll start a civil war. I thought you of all Elves would understand that. Especially after saying Vylok the Necromancer did not represent the views of the Elven population.'

'I meant no disrespect,' said Selouteau, holding her hand out to disarm the situation. 'Perhaps we should rest. It's late, and we will need sleep before tomorrow.'

'Yes, agreed,' said the Prince, before bidding his goodnight. Clapping Wilhelm on the shoulder, he strode to the doorway, then paused. 'I trust your lodgings will be comfortable tonight. I apologise, we are unable to provide anything of higher quality.'

'The bedding will be more than sufficient for a few hours of rest,' said Selouteau.

With the Prince's departure, Wilhelm led them to a small room littered with thin bedrolls, all tucked in with a patchwork of linen. He then described the location of the privy and bid his own goodnight, leaving Selouteau to wonder if tomorrow would be the beginning of the next Belissian war.

CHAPTER SEVEN

ᏟᎦ

SELOUTEAU WOKE BEFORE sunrise, trusting her body to know the time of day without the light of the twin suns to go by. Hearing no movement outside the chamber, she worked through a sequence of stretches and holds. Then, washing away the last fingers of fatigue with a splash of water, she pulled on her polished golden cuirass.

Her mind worked through the day's likely scenarios as she tied the golden armour over her officer's uniform. Ensuring the cuirass' broad, pointed shoulders and collar fit, she checked her polished black boots for any imperfection before pulling them on. Fastening her long, thin sword to her left side, she stood in the doorway and faced the still sleeping Elves.

'I'm going to count back from one hundred, and before I reach zero, you will be dressed and ready for the day,' she announced to her still sleeping crew. 'One hundred. Ninety-nine, ninety-eight, ninety-seven …'

Drowsy eyed and slack jawed, they jumped to their feet, tripping over each other in a rush to pull their uniforms over their undergarments. Selouteau turned her back on them to allow some modicum of privacy as they scrambled. 'Eighty-nine, eighty-eight ...'

Over her shoulder, she heard Perch swear before Wread's armour crashed to the stone. She continued counting, 'Thirty-six, thirty-five, thirty-four ...'

When she had the count of eight remaining, the scuffling behind her stopped, and she turned expectantly. Standing to attention, they were dressed and armoured for a day of battle.

Perch wore his usual black leather wrappings, their lightweight protection allowing him flexibility and a wide range of movement. The hilts of two swords protruded over his shoulders from where they were sheathed down his lithe back. A utility belt stocked full of useful tools circled his waist, and an assortment of throwing knives was spread over his left thigh.

Lieutenant Wread—a true officer of the Elven Armada—displayed his own silvery uniform. Broad, pointed shoulder pads and a collar smaller than Selouteau's bracketed his dark eyes, blond hair and serious expression. The bloodstains from the Ez's infirmary were hidden beneath his golden cuirass.

'Excellent timing. If you'll follow me ...' She marched from their chamber onto the cave system's main walkway. Knowing where she was after having memorised Ezell's maps, Selouteau turned toward

Ezguard via the long straight tunnel and set a brisk march. They moved swiftly, yet quietly.

'Did we need to have so little rest?' Perch rubbed his eyes, then pointed as they passed a room full of sleeping Ez. 'They're still sleeping.'

'They are not Elves. We are upholding our race's dignity.'

'Or our arrogance,' he snorted. 'You want to be there waiting when the Prince arrives.'

'It shows commitment.'

'It shows a lack of sleep,' he groaned.

Selouteau brought their brisk pace to a halt before a thick wooden door that barred the way ahead. It had solid timbers that were dark with age and pitted by wood grubs. But despite the pockmarks, Selouteau recognised a solid construction and its obvious intent: a siege door, designed to keep attackers out and nobles in.

She was again impressed at the Ez's ingenuity. The entire underground system of caves was constructed with a careful consideration Selouteau wouldn't have attributed to the Ez. She reflected on the Prince's words, wondering if the stronghold's purpose was to protect the Ez from the Elves, and if so, were there others just like it?

'Captain, have you noticed anything strange about the Ez who escorted us into the caves?' said Perch.

Selouteau searched Perch's expressions for answers. 'You mean Wilhelm? What about him?'

He leaned close and lowered his voice to a whisper. 'He is a Truthseer.'

'That's impossible, and you know it.'

'It isn't.'

Selouteau shook her head. 'Impossible. It is an Elven power along with mancery. No other Belissian race has the control required for mancery or Truthseeing.'

'What if I told you that isn't true?'

'The power lies in our blood alone. Never have the Ez shown an ability for Truthseeing, and they never will. It's in *our* blood,' she repeated as if to convince him.

'What evidence do you have, Ensign?' said Wread, stepping forward.

Perch glanced over his shoulder guardedly before speaking. 'When Wilhelm found us and led us into the caves, I found him intriguing so I reached out to him—'

'I told you not to use your Truthseeing,' said Selouteau.

'He was so certain we wouldn't attack, like he *knew* we wouldn't attack. And the panther he rides, there's a connection between them. It's as if they speak to each other.'

'That's absurd.'

'And he knew you were lying, Captain,' Perch continued.

'Excuse me.' Selouteau felt her tone change in defence.

'You lied about the Councils sending us here. He knew and signalled the Prince.'

She crossed her arms, both defensive and unconvinced.

'And what about the soldiers here?' Perch looked between Selouteau and Wread, who wore a 'you're-on-your-own' expression. 'How would the Prince have known who to trust? How would a prince as young as he have reached out to all those soldiers without revealing himself to the King?'

As she opened her mouth to comment, Perch cut her off and continued, 'But if Wilhelm is a Truthseer, the soldiers would be blind to the purpose of his questions, and he wouldn't reveal the intention until he was certain they would join. And when I questioned the Prince on how he did it, Wilhelm became uncomfortable. He wouldn't look anyone in the eyes and changed the topic—quickly,' said Perch.

'It still seems impossible, Ensign Perch. If he's a Truthseer, where would the power have come from—'

The heavy beat of boots marching in unison interrupted their conversation. Prince Ezell and his soldiers were approaching.

'Just keep an eye on him,' Selouteau added. Moving herself in front of Perch and Wread to greet the approaching Prince and his entourage, she spoke quickly over her shoulder. 'If he is what you think, then he will likely reveal more evidence. And if he is a Truthseer—which is impossible—then he will know you are probing his mind.'

'I'm better than that,' said Perch.

'No more probing. Visual observation only,' she emphasised.

'Understood, Captain.'

Ezell strolled into view, his young features belying his lack of sleep. Behind him, a group of Ez soldiers and muscled panthers padded. The beasts crouched under the tunnel's low ceiling, but even in the confines of the passage, they moved gracefully. Ezell led his mount with a slack rein clutched in one hand, his other resting lightly on the broadsword at his left hip.

'Wilhelm is here,' whispered Perch, as the Ez drew to a halt.

'Good morning! Have you been waiting long?' said Prince Ezell.

'Not long ... I see you're outfitted for battle today,' said Selouteau, switching to the Ez language and indicating the Prince's crimson armour. It was darker than the scarlet of the Royal Guard's armour and without any of the black highlights. The deep red colour sharply contrasted with the Prince's blond hair and pale blue eyes.

'I think a real leader should lead the charge, not hide behind troops making uninformed decisions,' said Prince Ezell.

'While I agree, we shouldn't be expecting a battle today. This mission is about stopping a war, not starting one,' said Selouteau.

'I have no intention of starting a war today, Captain Selouteau, but it doesn't hurt to be prepared,' said the Prince. He indicated the tunnel ahead of them. 'Shall we?'

The three Elves allowed the Prince and his giant panther to pass. Ezell produced a key and unlocked the aged timber door with a resonant thunk. On heavy hinges it swung outwards, revealing a featureless tunnel beyond. Selouteau strained to see ahead, but the rock floor, walls and ceiling were indistinguishable in the gloom.

Grabbing an unlit oil lantern from a stack beside the door, Ezell lit it on a burning wall lamp. 'Take a lantern each and please make yourself comfortable in the middle of the pack. It's roughly seven hours walk to Ezguard.'

They trudged in silence. The surrounding stone was oppressive, and the air was stale. Unable to see anything past the panther ahead and the one directly behind, Selouteau was forced to watch the featureless walls roll past.

She realised with growing ire they could have marched on loop for hours and she would be none the wiser. There were no markers or measurements displaying how far they'd come or how far it was to their destination. The constant weight of the stone taxed her patience. She hated being confined like this. It darkened her thoughts until all she could think about was the weight of stone above her. She longed to be on the deck of her airship, far above the land, limitless freedom in her grasp, and the wind in her hair …

'Captain?' said Perch, matching pace beside her.

She could hear the concern in his voice but shook her head in response; she didn't feel like dealing with his targeted questions right now. She wasn't in the mood.

Warm emotions swirled within her mind, and she began to feel distant from the passage's darkness. She felt a soft glow infiltrate her thoughts and wash away the ire, until she realised what the Truthseer was doing: he was lending his Truthseeing—as he had in Gusting—to lift her mood.

'What are you doing?' she said.

'It was expertly done,' the Truthseer winked. She felt his mind brush hers as he spoke directly to her thoughts. *'Not even one of my own would have felt that.'*

'Your cockiness will be your undoing.' She thought into the link he'd created between their minds.

'Remember, I told you how to block your mind, Selouteau. Concentrate on a wall and think of nothing else.'

Selouteau concentrated and constructed a wall of stone around her thoughts. Immediately, Perch's lingering presence disappeared.

'See. Just like that,' said Perch.

Selouteau frowned, but she could feel her lips twitching into a smile. Had the Truthseer just proved that she could block him from her mind? Was that even possible?

Her thoughts began to race: if the Truthseers no longer had the power to read minds, how would they ensure the Councils' wills were enacted? How would the Elves then police Belissia, and how would the Councils be held accountable for their actions? Suddenly, Selouteau wondered if the Traditionalist regime was unravelling in more ways than anyone realised ...

Before she had time to consider any further about what Perch had just shown her, Selouteau saw a three-way fork appear in the tunnel ahead. Without pause, they proceeded down the left tunnel and shortly after met a noticeable incline in the passageway. After another two hours of walking, her mind still racing at the possibilities of what Perch had shown her, Selouteau's boots connected with a flight of rough-hewn steps cut into the bedrock. They led upwards into the darkness at a sharp angle.

'The stone here is different,' said Perch, running his hand along the wall as he climbed the steps behind her. 'We must be under Ezguard.'

At three-hundred and fifty steps, Selouteau stopped counting as they thankfully topped a landing. The stone here was redder than in the caves, and the air smelt dustier. She followed the Prince and his soldiers beneath a strong, brick buttress—

the first sign of civilisation since leaving the caves seven hours prior. They stepped onto another flat, uninteresting passage, though this one was noticeably neater in the way it was carved from the stone.

'We're here,' said the Prince, halting before what looked like a solid wall made from the same bricks as the buttress. It seemed out of place in the passage carved directly from the bedrock.

Sliding his hand into a recess hidden within the buttressing, the Prince triggered a mechanism that clunked in response. The sound of stone grating stone then reached Selouteau's ears, and the solid wall slid aside.

They passed beneath the new opening into what appeared to be the dungeons of Ezguard. The smell—nauseating—assaulted her nose and brought tears to her eyes.

'Not decaying dungeon smells again,' said Perch. Covering his nose and speaking in Elven, the Truthseer whispered to Selouteau: 'Is this a bad time for a joke about the smells of the Lesser Races?'

She silenced him with a look and followed the group out of the cell onto a stone walkway that ran the length of the cell blocks. The half-dozen cells were all empty, which surprised Selouteau, though the pungent smell told her they were only recently emptied.

They continued through the dank, empty cell block and onto the dungeon's main access-way. Treading quickly down its length, they climbed another set of stairs into what appeared to be the undercroft of

Ezguard's citadel. There, the hallways widened, brightened and grew taller. And though they left the dungeons' reek, the floors, walls and ceiling here were all constructed with the same bleak stone.

Prince Ezell quickened their pace until they jogged the lengthy corridors and bounded up the curving staircases, moving ever upwards through the castle.

Following in the middle of the pack, Selouteau maintained their pace easily. She hoped the young Prince knew what he was doing. She didn't yet feel anxious, but her battle-honed instincts ensured she assessed and reassessed every possibility. Exits, hiding places, the likely position of medical supplies and the best location for an ambush all added themselves to the mental map she created as they went. She knew if all else failed, she could navigate her way back to the tunnels under pressure. Of course, Selouteau hoped the morning would continue as expected but remained keenly aware that plans seldom proceeded as expected, especially when an enemy was involved.

They passed no one in the lower levels, and as they continued to climb through the citadel's undercroft, Selouteau wondered why the hallways were empty. Surely, the castle would be bustling with servers, maids and all manner of other personnel at all times of the day. She wondered if the Prince had arranged for their path to be deserted.

Selouteau followed the soldiers into a large open corridor, its high vaulted ceiling and columned walls far grander than anything they'd passed through below. The Ez mounted their panthers and trotted down the polished marble floors.

They were rushing. Something didn't feel right. Selouteau shot Perch a concerned look and extending her stride, she moved up the ranks to run beside the Prince, who looked down from atop his panther.

'Welcome to Ezguard's citadel,' said Prince Ezell.

'What's the hurry?'

'If we're quick, we'll catch the Governor at morning tea before he signs the agreement. My men have told us they're dining as we speak.'

'That is not the plan, Prince Ezell. We were going to capture Thawn in his quarters, discreetly.'

'The plan has changed, Captain; he is no longer in his quarters. But we can still catch him.'

Selouteau opened her mouth to speak as they rounded the next corner, but the words died on her tongue. There was a company of Human soldiers across their path: it was an ambush.

CHAPTER EIGHT

ENSIGN PERCH SENSED the waiting Human soldiers far too late. They were arranged in ranks before the doors to the dining hall of Ezguard's citadel in an ambush. The soldiers carried weapons that looked like miniature versions of the cannons from Gusting, and together, they raised their weapons and fired.

Beams of white energy filled the air so fast that there was only a moment to react. Perch reached out with his Truthseeing and—infiltrating Prince Ezell's mind with ease—took control of the young man's body. To anyone watching, the Prince simply threw himself out of harm's way just in time. But the other Ez didn't react as quickly.

Screams filled the air, as the white energy smashed into Ez soldiers and black panthers alike. A wave of pain washed around the room with such force that Perch tried to close off his Truthseeing, lest the emotions swamp him.

He watched as Ez soldiers and panthers were gunned down in the onslaught, including Wilhelm's panther.

A spike of Truthseeing smashed into Perch's mind with a strength that he that wasn't expecting. Looking for the source, he watched as Wilhelm's panther was gunned down under the onslaught. The great beast slipped on the marble floor and fell into a tangled mess of limbs, howling in pain as it tried to get back up. But the Truthseeing spike hadn't come only from the creature. Its rider rolled from his saddle, screaming as the bolts of white energy ploughed into his panther's body.

And suddenly, feeling the young Ez and beast screaming as one, Perch knew for certain he'd been right. *'He is a Truthseer,'* Perch screamed across a link to Selouteau. *'He's sharing a mind link with his panther.'*

Without the time to revel in his victory, Perch ducked as the Humans begun targeting the other Royal Guards. More white energy filled the air, as the Prince's men howled, and their panthers floundered on the marble floors, scrambling to escape.

Perch moved. The plan was a disaster. He had to get to Selouteau, free her and make their escape before it got worse. Dodging stray beams, Perch pushed the nearest Human aside and looked for Wread. He spotted the Aquamancer in the opposite direction from the Captain and made his decision. Perch ran for Selouteau: his priority.

Zigzagging through the battle, he made a line for the Captain. He dodged and feinted around the Human soldiers. They were far too slow to touch him, and any that were in his way, he simply barrelled through them.

The stench of burning flesh and melted hair assaulted his nostrils, and he could feel the distress building inside Wilhelm's mind. Perch had seen this kind of reaction before. When a young Truthseer was struck with grief and didn't know the power they held, they could be incredibly dangerous.

He reached out to the young Ez with his Truthseeing in the hope of easing that pain, but Wilhelm's pain lashed out against his mind with such force that Perch's knees buckled. He fell in a heap and was immediately grabbed by the surrounding Humans. They piled on him, throwing their weight atop him, thinking that he wouldn't be able to escape.

A commanding voice sliced through the noise. 'Cease fire and stay down!'

The steady beat of weapon fire ceased, and was replaced by the groans of downed Ez, the ragged breathing of wounded panthers and Wilhelm's anguished sobs.

Perch allowed the soldiers to drag him forward beside Selouteau and Wread. The Human soldiers shoved the Elves to their knees and jammed the snouts of their weapons into the back of their heads.

Perch knew they couldn't be the ones to start the war, so he waited to see how Selouteau wanted to proceed, as a pair of boots echoed on the stone floor. Perch felt a new mind enter the scene.

A short, fat Human male walked forward from the dining hall. His belly bulged against a white uniform, and an array of colourful medals were plastered across his sagging breast. The man clasped his hands behind his back and cleared his throat with a self-satisfied look. He then spoke in the Ez language, though with a terrible accent that showed how new he was to the language.

'I anticipated the Prince in Exile would intrude on these peaceful negotiations,' the fat Human man called so everyone could hear, but he looked to Ezell, who was helping an injured Ez sit upright against a column, 'and so, you'll be happy to know, Prince Ezell, that your father and I signed the treaty last night. The Ez are now the newest members of the Human Alliance.'

Perch's mind reeled as he watched Prince Ezell pat his panther to stay, before picking his way over the fallen bodies. Aware of the weapons trained on him, the Prince held up his hands as he faced the fat Human. 'Where is my father?'

The Human grinned, and Perch felt a swell of self-importance from the man as he spoke. 'Your father was very upset at your exile. Perhaps even more so when he realised how many Royal Guards defected with you. It was my idea to spread word of today's signing in the hope it would lure you out … And here you are. I argued hard for you, Prince Ezell, convincing your father that all young men feel the need to push boundaries. The treaty states no punishment for you and your loyal Ez, for I believe loyalty should be nurtured. Of course, you'll have to return to Ezguard and accept your place in the Human Alliance.'

Perch's mind ran through the possibilities. The plan to sneak in and force the Governor to accept a new treaty should have worked: his own Truthseeing would have ensured the Governor's compliance. But that was not an option now. Even with the Captain and Wread's mancery, he knew they were vastly outnumbered, and he'd seen what the Human weapons could do …

Perhaps he should've looked into the Prince's thoughts sooner, and if he'd been younger, he would have. But as much as it pained him to admit it, Selouteau was right. They had no way of knowing the extent of Wilhelm's power, and the chance was too high that Wilhelm would sense Perch picking through the Prince's thoughts. And with the current political position, Perch had no intention of destroying their chances with the Ez. Selouteau's orders were to gain allies, not start another war. And his orders were to watch and protect, not interfere.

Perch looked at Governor Thawn and realised another opportunity had presented itself. He reached out to the Governor's mind and found it ordered but zealous. Unwavering in his personal righteousness, he truly believed in his Divine-King and in the holy mission he had been entrusted with. Images of scorching white flames and soaring ceilings flashed through

Perch's mind, and between the towering columns of white light, he saw soldiers, hundreds of thousands of soldiers, all marching in unison.

The Governor continued. 'How you choose to proceed, Prince Ezell, will determine whether you're branded a hero or a criminal … so think well.' Governor Thawn then turned his attention to where Perch, Wread and Selouteau were now held by the Human soldiers. 'You, Elves, are now trespassing in violation of Ezguard's newest laws. Your kind is no longer welcome here.' Thawn tilted his head and focused his eyes on something the others could not see. 'We came here in search of holy artefacts, and instead, we found Belissians crushed under the Elven rule. Let this serve as a warning to the Elves.' He waved a hand to encompass the scene before him. 'No longer will you be allowed your tyranny.'

'Does the Ez King know you have thousands of troops waiting in Gusting?' said Selouteau.

Thawn glanced at her. 'Of course he does, Elf. I do not keep things from my allies. He knows I brought troops to protect myself from the possibility of a hostile reception.'

Perch could feel Selouteau's incredulity when she replied, 'Hostile reception? You shot down our airships! It was you who fired the first shot.'

'A lie,' Thawn replied, making a strange symbol across his chest with his hand. 'A noble heart shall not bear a lie from a basal tongue.' The words fell from his lips with the weight of a religious act.

Around the room, Humans repeated the act, performing the identical movement over their hearts.

Perch could feel the unshakeable Truth behind the Governor's words and knew that the Humans truly believed in everything their Divine-King stood for.

'Now,' the Governor said, his beady eyes searching Selouteau's face, 'you must be Captain Selouteau, the Elf who attacked Gusting and killed my men. I have to give you my thanks.'

The men holding Selouteau—who had been wrinkling their noses in disgust at the Elf—looked at their Governor in surprise. And Selouteau pulled back as far as the weapons pressed to her head would allow. 'What for?'

'Your attack on Gusting killed dozens and maimed countless more of my soldiers, which is unforgivable. Were circumstances different, I would execute you … but I want to thank you, because you maimed me too.' He unclasped his arms from behind his back, and Perch looked to where the Governor's left arm should have been. Instead, the sleeve of his uniform had been rolled back to reveal a mechanical arm.

'Isn't it glorious?' said the Governor.

Similar in length and width to his good arm, cogs, pistons and linkages were visible within the machine arm's depths, their motions open to the air. It had the resemblance of the inner working of a clock, except that the appendage ended in three spindly fingers. Perch likened the fingers to the legs of the Rock Spiders that lurked in the cliffs surrounding the Cradle.

'King Ezette of the Ez tells me your sorcerous abilities are called mancery and that the Elves alone hold such destructive power. No wonder the rest of Belissia are afraid of you.' Thawn waited for a response from Selouteau, but she offered only a glare.

'Your explosion,' he pointed his clockwork arm at Selouteau with a whir of spinning cogs, 'tore my arm to pieces. The doctors worked hard, saying my only hope of survival was to amputate the arm. There was so much blood, I thought I was going to die ... I kept thinking I was going to die at the hands of an enemy I'd never seen—'

'Did you have your eyes closed when you tortured the Ambassador?' blurted Wread. Perch could see childhood memories playing across Wread's mind, his thoughts clearly agitated. Perch gave the Aquamancer a wave of calming emotion; the last thing they needed was for Wread to cause a scene they would regret.

Governor Thawn continued as if not interrupted '... but I was saved by the good grace of our Divine-King. He travelled all the way from our homeland to thank me. Told me I had worked hard to further the Human crusade and that he was going to give me another chance. And so, he fashioned me this arm as a tribute to his power and generosity, for serving him with my life.'

'Unfortunately, you're still alive,' Wread interrupted again.

Thawn's attention returned to the room. 'You Elves are very rude. I am alive by the grace of our Divine-King,' he declared, thrusting his arm into the air.

'The Eternal Divine-King,' the Human soldiers chorused in unison, 'Armageddon's Saviour.'

Perch stared at the surrounding Humans, his brows raised in surprise. His first thought was that they'd been captured by a cult, and the second was that the soldiers were all speaking the Ez language, which didn't seem possible given that they'd landed only a few weeks prior. He filed the information for later consideration.

'So I must thank you, Captain Selouteau,' Thawn continued. 'Without your intervention, I would never have received such a beautiful gift from the Divine-King. It is a shame I cannot show you all of its tricks today—as much as you deserve it—so instead, you'll go free and carry a message back to your Councils: a warning. "Cease your tyranny and leave, or you will feel the full might of the Divine-King's justice."'

'No,' said Selouteau, and Perch could feel her mancery building in her belly. 'You fired the first shot, Governor. You blew our airships out of the sky.'

Governor Thawn looked down at her with an expression of a teacher schooling a child. 'The Elves fired upon us first and killed three of my men. We simply acted in self-defence.'

Selouteau opened her mouth to reply but stumbled. Perch could feel her internal struggle. *Was it possible? Could the Elves have attacked the Humans first?*

Perch knew it was entirely possible—in fact highly likely. He knew better than most about the conflicts started and won by the Elven Councils. Though Selouteau thought he was a new Truthseer, Perch had spent centuries learning of the darker sides of Belissia's wars, where the Elves had easily turned to bloodshed when the need arose. With each and every escalation, he'd witnessed firsthand how the Elven Councils were masters of war and, indeed, masters of Belissia. He reached out to the Governor's mind and could see that he spoke the Truth. The Humans had fired in self-defence. Someone from the Elven Councils had started the war.

Perch felt Selouteau analysing the reports she'd read from the Councils: 'airships shot down during scouting mission over newly occupied terrain'. Because of those very words, Selouteau had volunteered herself for the Ambassador's extraction. She'd seen it as a chance to show her military prowess, prove she was the daughter of the Grand Admiral and the Great Inquisitor. But now Perch sensed a shift in Selouteau. She wondered if she'd played directly into the Councils' hands, something Perch knew as the Truth. She was their unwitting pawn in producing another excuse for war.

He watched her thoughts darken as she wondered if the entire Elven rule was built on a web of lies, an entwining mess of deceits all designed to maintain control. And although she hadn't admitted as much to Perch, she didn't believe in the return of the Purge anymore. As Perch had suggested, it was too convenient and too ambiguous, and other than the ramblings of the oldest Elves, no proof of it existed.

Governor Thawn laughed aloud, a rolling chortle that echoed about the hall. 'See! You cannot deny it's possible that the Elves fired first.'

The Governor moved to speak again, but a groan from Wilhelm's panther interrupted him. The beast made a gurgling sound that came from deep in its throat, its broken body still sprawled across the marble floor. Although the Human soldiers remained motionless with weapons trained on the captives, their focus was drawn to the panther.

Wilhelm stroked his dying panther's head between sobs. Despite his mental barriers, Wilhelm's misery pushed against Perch's consciousness with a power that impressed him more than he'd have thought possible. It was a power many would believe only an Elf could possess … even if he knew better.

Perch reached out with his mind to lend comfort to the great beast in her last moments of life. He brushed the panther's consciousness, ready to offer support, but the creature was all but gone. The intelligent consciousness he'd sensed connected with

Wilhelm before was no more, and now her mind clung hopelessly to fear and pain.

'Will somebody help me?' Wilhelm begged. 'Please ...'

Nobody moved. Perch sensed their apprehension, every person unsure what they could do to help the great beast. Her fur was marred with wounds from the Human's energy weapons, and a pool of blood had begun to form on the floor.

'... anyone?' Wilhelm pleaded.

Lieutenant Wread stood, and immediately every eye in the room snapped to his movement. Human weapons were raised and pointed at him. The Aquamancer held out his hands and approached Wilhelm. 'I'm a healer. Let me see what I can do to help.'

Treading through the pool of blood, Wread walked around the panther and knelt at the great beast's legs, his back to the Governor. The Aquamancer ran his hands over Zethish's body, and the creature made a gurgling sound in its throat. Wread spoke: 'Tell me, Governor Thawn, what excuse do you have for torturing and killing the Ambassador?'

'Can you help her?' Wilhelm asked Lieutenant Wread, his face streaked with tears.

The Aquamancer's gaze softened towards Wilhelm, and with the barest movement, he shook his head. He took Wilhelm's hand and led him around the panther's bulk to where he crouched at the beast's back. 'I said, what excuse do you have for torturing and killing Ambassador Tendallanon?'

Perch watched Wread's hands move over the dying beast, but Perch could tell it was a trick. He stretched his mind towards Selouteau and said, '*I think Lieutenant Wreadallanon is about to do something really quite stupid.*'

'The Elven Ambassador was an assassin sent to kill me,' said the Governor. 'But he failed and suffered the consequences.'

'My brother was not an assassin,' snapped Wread.

Perch could feel the healer's mancery bubbling below the surface of his control.

Governor Thawn looked thoughtful. 'Your *brother* tried to murder me in my—'

'LIAR!'

Perch braced himself, as Wread called upon his Aquamancy. The pool of blood flooded across the floor and gathered under the healer's hand into a ball of roiling liquid. He then snapped it into a whip that he flicked across the room to where it cracked across the Governor's chest. The Human screamed as he fell backwards into his men, and blood poured from the deep gash where the Aquamancy had torn through his clothing and skin.

Immediately, the room fell into chaos: some Human soldiers tripped and fell under their Governor's weight, and those that were left standing opened fire.

Lieutenant Wread redrew the blood whip and spread it into a flat disk that floated before him. He then jammed himself and the distraught Wilhelm deeper against the dead panther's back and took cover.

Perch watched the blood shield hiss and bubble as it absorbed the bolts of weapon fire and grimaced at the putrid smell of boiling blood. From across the hall, he could feel Wread's black emotions.

More than anything, Wread wanted to end Thawn for what he'd done to his brother. He wanted to use his Aquamancy to drain the blood from the Governor's veins. But in spite of his extreme hatred, Perch could feel the healer's cool logic pervading. He could feel Wread's mind acknowledging that if he continued the attack right now, they would likely all die. And he could feel Wread understanding he wouldn't win if his crewmates perished as collateral.

Even though the Humans were still firing at the Aquamancer, Perch felt relief for Wread, but his elation was short-lived, as another mind, sharp and abrasive, cut through his mental space.

'You killed her!' Wilhelm's anguish burst through the noise of the firing weapons. 'YOU KILLED HER!' he screamed again, and his mind shot outwards. It was like the probing of a Truthseer's ability, like a blade piercing his skull.

Perch recoiled and clasped his hands to his head, the sudden impact of Wilhelm's mind smashing its way into his thoughts. Squeezing his head against the pain, Perch saw Wilhelm's Truthseeing hit Human, Ez and Elf alike; Human soldiers stumbled, Ez clasped their heads, and Wread's control of his Aquamancy failed, so litres of blood splashed across the floor.

Blood poured over Wilhelm, who threw his head back and screamed incomprehensible words. A torrent of emotion surged outwards from Wilhelm, swamping every mind in the hallway. Ranks of Humans fell writhing to the floor. Ez riders slipped from their mounts and landed awkwardly across the polished tiles, arms and legs twisting this way and that. All of them clawed at their scalps and faces to stop the pain, howling in unison with Wilhelm, whose Truthseeing flared with each additional man's agony.

Perch dragged himself across the mass of flailing bodies. He'd endured all kinds of training at the hands of the Truthseers, but he'd never felt raw power like this.

He needed nearly all of his concentration just to barricade his mind as he inched his way towards Captain Selouteau. Climbing over Human and Ez alike, Perch made his way across the sea of writhing bodies. She had been right next to him, but it felt like an eternity with Wilhelm's mind pressing down on him. When finally he reached Selouteau, her eyes were wide and staring as she screamed in unending torture. Perch placed his hands around her face and willed what was left of his own Truthseeing into her mind.

'*Let me help,*' he whispered in thought, surrounding her mind protectively with his own. '*Think of your barriers, Selouteau. I can help block your mind, but I need your help.*'

He felt something shift within her thoughts, and together, they blocked out Wilhelm's Truthseeing.

Suddenly, her eyes cleared. She took a deep, long breath and spoke hoarsely when she met his gaze. 'Thank you, Ensign.'

Perch grabbed her broad shoulders, and together they helped each other upright. 'Selouteau … Captain, we need to get out of here.'

'The Governor …'

'It's too late, the Ez have signed the treaty. We have to escape and report to the Councils.' Perch looked over his shoulder at Wilhelm, standing amid the writhing bodies. 'I need your help. Wread and the Prince—we can't leave them here. And about Wilhelm … I told you so.' The statement felt hollow, even to him, because he knew the implications of Wilhelm's Truthseeing, and he knew what *his* orders would be. The Councils would kill the young Ez. His power threatened their control. 'We need to get Wilhelm back to the Truthseers.'

Selouteau leaned heavily on him as she stood and surveyed the scene, and he could feel control entering her thoughts. 'Can you hold him back long enough for us to escape?' She had to shout to be heard above the screams of those around them.

'Of course.'

'He's so much stronger than—'

'Yes, but I can render him unconscious when we're far enough away, so they won't recover in time to give chase.'

Together, they moved forward. Even with Perch's Truthseeing and Selouteau's help blocking her mind, they could feel Wilhelm's emotion buffeting them like a gale. With every step, their footing was threatened by a fresh wave of Truthseeing that promised to knock them stumbling to the floor.

They reached Wilhelm's dead panther, Zethish, and Perch took note of where Wread and the Prince were. The blond Ez had crawled backwards to lie in a crumpled heap at his panther's feet, where green luminescent eyes watched guardedly over the suffering rider.

'*The panthers are unharmed by Truthseeing,*' Perch whispered to Selouteau's mind, pointing out the panthers guarding their riders. '*We can use one to escape.*'

Nodding, Selouteau gestured to the convulsing Wread and yelled over the din. 'Can you help him?'

'*I'm barely keeping our minds…*'

'Then help me pick him up.'

They each took one of Wread's flailing arms and dragged the bloodied Elf, kicking and screaming, across the floor to the Prince and his mount. Though unable to hear over the cacophony of screaming, Perch was sure he heard the beast growl a warning. He motioned Selouteau to stop and reached towards the panther with his mind, brushing against its consciousness. He fought with the Truthseeing he had left and showed the beast images of escaping to safety. Releasing the link with a slump of his shoulders and the onset of a spinning headache, he looked into the panther's eyes and hoped he saw understanding.

He looked again at the bloodied Wilhelm. The young Ez's power still washed over the area in formidable waves, but Perch felt his hold begin to slacken. *'Captain, Wilhelm's faltering. We need to get out!'*

Selouteau heaved Wread and the Prince onto the panther's back, where they continued to writhe. She lashed them to saddle, then handed the reins to Perch. 'I'll get Wilhelm.'

Perch nodded, tugging at the reins to pull the panther down the hallway towards their escape. Selouteau waded across the bodies towards Wilhelm, in the opposite direction.

Wilhelm's mind filled the hall around them, but Perch knew, with such a state of Truthseeing, he would be disconnected from his body, unaware of what was happening to his physical form. Selouteau reached the young Ez and threw him over her shoulder. Perch was impressed that even that close to Wilhelm's power, Selouteau could maintain her blocks.

She staggered slightly and caught his eye.

'Run!'

CHAPTER NINE

'I'VE COLLAPSED THE tunnel behind us, but that will only buy us a few hours,' said Ezell, as he paced the small cave. The plan had failed. His father had signed the treaty with the Humans, and he would be branded a criminal. A true exile. The Elves had rescued him and brought him back to these caves, but they needed to act. He needed to act. 'We need to leave these caves before the Humans get here.'

'Agreed,' said Captain Edric, the only other Ez in the room. 'That is our highest priority right now. But after fleeing Ezguard, where will we go?'

'Well, we can't go south,' Ezell said, pushing his blond hair out of his face. 'The Humans are at Gusting, and the Gavidgeon soldiers are the best in the realm. Wilhelm's father, Count Torla, is loyal to my father and the crown. If he hears of our passage through his county, he'll hunt us down for sure.'

'We could stay deep within the Western County. We could hide,' said Edric.

'And get eaten alive by the beasts? I don't think so,' said Prince Ezell.

Captain Edric ticked the options off on his fingers: 'We can't go east, the Human airships will spot us from the sky, so we'd never make it across the Blue Plains. And we can't go west, for no one has crossed the Border Ranges and returned from the Sand Tribes of Ver Dunn.'

Ezell frowned. 'The Sand Tribes of Ver Dunn are just fairy tales, Edric. But still, we can't go west— the Border Ranges are barren, and I've heard there's nothing but wastelands beyond. We have only one option, and we'll have to move swiftly.'

'And what about the soldiers you left behind in Ezguard for the Governor, my Prince? What do you think he will do to them?'

Ezell whirled on the Captain. 'I don't know what he'll do to them, but right now, we need to focus on escaping.'

'Every one of them will be branded criminals, my Prince.'

'They all made their decisions, for one reason or another, Edric … just as you did. Of course, I want to rescue them, but right now, we need to make our escape. My father's and the Governor's troops could be on their way as we speak, and it's only a day's ride from Ezguard. Our only protection is the difficulty of finding this entrance from the Western County. We have to hope that slows them down.'

'They could have used the Human airships to get here. We have no idea how fast they are.'

'I hadn't thought of that … Our decision is made: we're heading north,' said Prince Ezell.

'North! To what … the Elves?' said Edric. 'When have the Elves ever done anything good for us?'

'They rescued me from the Governor.'

'That doesn't make up for millenia of abuse. What if your father is right and—'

'No.' Ezell raised a silencing finger. 'Stay behind and wait if you think the Humans are better than the Elves.'

'You know I didn't mean it like that.'

'Well, I'm not sure anymore.' Ezell threw up his hands. 'This is not how I thought it would happen. I thought a political exile would change my father's mind, and then everything would go back to normal. That he would welcome me back … but now, this.' Ezell clenched his fists as his emotions boiled.

'You could hand yourself in and say it was all a big misunderstanding. You could tell the Humans that the Elves took you under duress.'

Ezell collapsed in an uncomfortable chair and hung his head. 'And then what? Play the pretty Prince and live the rest of my life under the Human rule?'

Edric sighed and moved to stand beside Ezell. 'We don't know anything about the Human Alliance, my Prince. It could be wonderful, for all we know. They might even have a princess for you to marry.'

Ezell rolled his eyes. 'You know my tastes lay elsewhere, Edric. I have no interest in marrying a woman. Argh! I feel like my father has run from one tyranny to another; except this time, he's given them the right to legitimise their reign.' He wiped his eyes—not crying yet, but they were wet. 'I can't go back. The Ez won't live under oppression from any race. We have to be free to make our own choices.'

'Spoken like a true Prince of the Ez.' Edric smiled warmly and placed his hands on Ezell's young shoulders. 'The soldiers followed your exile because they trusted in you, Prince Ezell. We believe the Ez deserve their own lives, free from the Elves and the Humans, and we see you as our best chance for that future.'

'Inspiring words laden with pressure,' said Ezell.

The Captain smiled and then spoke softly. 'If we go north, where will we hide?'

'We can use the Rift for cover in case the Humans send their airships.'

'What about the beasts in the Rift?'

'If we stick closer to the Rift walls, there's a good chance we can move unharmed,' said the Prince.

'A good chance … where will we go?' said Edric.

'To Chancy in the Northern County.'

'Chancy? But Count Tobias Borlonn is a pacifist and detests the idea of war. How do you think he will receive us when he realises we are enemies of the crown,' said Edric.

'There's an Ez royal contact in Chancy who communicates with the Elves; there's one in every major city. In Chancy its a man called Defolt, if I remember correctly. He will make contact with the Elves, and we can ask for their help. I think now is as good a time as any. Our options are limited,' said Prince Ezell.

'Captain Selouteau could have taken us with them instead of leaving us here in the middle of this mess.'

'They had their own concerns,' said Prince Ezell.

'Chancy is more than a week's ride from here, my Prince, especially if we're hiding in the Rift to avoid airships. What will we do once we get there? We can't exactly waltz through the front door.'

'We'll send scouts ahead. The land around Chancy is mountainous and full of rocky outcrops. Perhaps we can find another cave to hide in,' said Prince Ezell.

'Just like real criminals,' said Edric.

Within the hour, Ezell and his troops had cleared the cave of everything they could carry. The ever-efficient Edric, true to his former role as Captain of the Royal Guard, ensured every Ez held only the essentials for their escape northbound. Each soldier took only a week's portion of food, weapons and the armour on their backs.

As the troops prepared to leave, Ezell scanned the skies from beneath the rocky overhang, his chest tight with apprehension: he watched for the arrival of the Human airships. There were none to be seen, and yet, the creeping sensation that they were on their way lingered in his mind.

Edric led the evacuation calmly. He sent the riders into the forests of the Western County in groups of eight. When only half the troop's number remained, he then motioned for the Prince to join the next group: he was safest with the middle of the escaping soldiers.

Edric gave the command, and Ezell, with the other riders spurred his panther into a gallop, raced across the hard ground before ploughing into the thick undergrowth of the Western County. Though the twin suns' heat beat down on the Prince in his crimson armour, the cool air beneath the tall trees and the air whipping at his face kept it bearable.

Trunks whizzed past, and trusting his panther, Boolen, to thread himself along the path without guidance, Ezell kept his eyes skyward. He scanned for signs of the approaching Human airships, as an uncomfortable feeling swelled in his gut.

They burst through a stand of brush and leapt straight into a stream full of clear, cold water. Crashing through the knee-high creek and spraying fountains every which way, they continued north. The plan was to follow the stream's meandering path in the hope of hiding their tracks.

As water cascaded around them, Ezell pondered the outcome of turning himself in to the Humans. He had lived his entire life safe within the bounds of his father's rule and had never felt uncertain about anything in his life; he'd never had reason to. But now, he felt as if nothing was certain: he could be attacked by a vicious Juian, captured by the Humans or even betrayed by one of his men at any moment. He was on the run as an exile from his own people.

Ezell breathed through his growing anxiety and wondered how real criminals could live like this. *It's exhausting,* he thought. Always on the run and always looking over their shoulder, waiting for the next attack ... He took a moment to steady his thoughts before they escaped his control, just as Edric had taught him.

His mind flicked to Edric.

For as long as the Prince could remember, Captain Edric had been there to watch over Ezell: his mentor, sword coach, friend, and confidant. On many occasions, Ezell had thought of Edric as more of a father than the King, who was busy running the Ez kingdom. Ezell had deeply respected the King, but as he'd grown older, he'd discovered they were often at odds. Ezell saw much room for improvement in the traditional ways of the Ez people. He'd grown into an active member in all state matters and had on several occasions questioned his father's decisions publicly. After many heated arguments and several public ordeals, the King ordered Ezell to no longer attend state matters. It was then when his father spoke of joining the Human Alliance that Ezell pronounced political exile—in the hope of forcing his father's hand. Ezell realised now how naive he had been.

Until that morning, Ezell had been driven by the certainty that he would return to Ezguard's citadel after thwarting the Humans' political takeover. He was certain he'd return a hero, proving to the King and the Ez people he was competent and ready to rule. But his plan had failed, and his father had signed the Ez into the Human Alliance, a decision that left Ezell breathless. How had his father been so easily convinced to join their Alliance? Would he ever have the chance to find out?

Before he could answer, the rider at the head of their group stopped in a shower of mist and darted under a broad stand of tree ferns. He waved frantically at the following Ez as he called: 'Airship!'

The Ez scattered for the trees—splashing water about in their haste—and Ezell directed Boolen to a stand of willows that were draping over the stream. They needed to hide.

Ezell's breathing quietened, as a low rumbling reverberated through the forest.

The noise grew louder, and soon the crackling of trees joined the approaching rumble. Several Royal Guards rested their hands on their weapons, their panthers lowering themselves into the cold water with tails flicking in agitation. Ezell turned his head toward the sound, and beneath him, Boolen tensed. It was coming.

Suddenly, the silhouette of a broad-bodied airship with glowing engines appeared overhead. Buckling trees in its wake, it poured heated air into the forest so that foliage scattered into a whirlwind around them. Hot air and leaf matter whipped at Ezell's face as he peered upwards at the massive contraption: its dark bulk was outlined against the bright blue sky, and there were gun emplacements along its length, panning back and forth in search.

Leaves and twigs whipped at his hair and bounced off his armour as the black metal hull glided overhead and headed west. Trees bent and swayed in the airship's wake, and as quickly as it had appeared, the airship left, the racket of its passage soon swallowed by the quiet burbling of the stream. The Prince sighed in relief and turned to his guards, their eyes wide with nervous exhilaration.

'That was close,' said Ezell to no one in particular.

'I've never seen an airship like that before,' nodded another guard.

The soldiers began muttering, and Ezell waded Boolen to the middle of the stream where he spoke over their hushed tones.

'We were lucky this time. Lucky that we received warning and there was enough room here for all of us to hide. We can't take that chance again. We need to be more vigilant for another airship's approach. And we need to move faster. Keep your ears open and look after each other. We have no idea how many airships are out here, but you can bet they are looking for us. We need to make the entrance to the Rift before nightfall.'

Ezell kicked Boolen forward. The panther leapt from the water through the ferns on the eastern bank and broke into a loping run. The Royal Guards took up positions behind and around him and together they charged onwards. Leaving the stream, they curved to the northeast.

Up through the canopy, Ezell could see the imposing structure of the Rift's entrance, the unmistakable cliff faces guiding him beneath the thick forest canopy. He allowed a brief smile to touch his lips, his earlier angst slipping away. Knowing the lumbering airships' loud engines would signal their approach left Ezell feeling far more confident of their escape. With the panthers' hearing, they had a good chance, and with a bit of luck, they would be out of the Western County before the suns set. They just had to get there, and hope they didn't meet any of the beasts from the Western County along the way.

Chapter Ten

EZELL'S HEAD WHIPPED left as a light chatter drifted through the dense forest around him. They were still fleeing through the Western County, but he couldn't see more than a few steps in any direction through the thick undergrowth; every sense in his body screamed danger at him. Boolen growled low in his throat, and in response, a soft grunt sounded from the opposite direction. For a moment, the forest was still, and as Ezell looked left and right, nothing moved.

Then the trees exploded with movement.

'Juians!' Ezell bellowed in warning to his men.

With razor claws, hairy arms and tooth-filled mouths, the Juians poured from the surrounding undergrowth. Bouncing off trunks and chittering loudly, the tiny creatures launched themselves with open mouths and sharply pointed teeth.

Boolen lunged and caught one of the furry, six-armed creatures in his jaws and ended its squealing life with a crunching spray of gore. Tossing the mess aside, the panther roared his defiance, as more Juians sprang from the foliage around them.

Ezell drew the broadsword from his left hip and sliced an airborne creature in half. To his left, an Ez rider screamed as their attackers dropped from the canopy above, landing on his shoulders and shredding his face with their talons. Riding the soldier's thrashing body to the ground, they chattered loudly and tore chunks of flesh from the Ez's face and neck as more attacked his panther. They ate the bloody chunks, as he gurgled and wheezed, drowning in his own blood.

Realising he wasn't wearing his own helmet, Ezell jerked it from the saddle behind him and tightened it over his face. Beneath him, Boolen lunged again, snatching another Juian from the air and crushing a second beneath his powerful paw.

Ezell's heart pounded as he swung his heavy sword; a right undercut, followed by an overhand twist. None of his training had prepared him for just how fast and ferocious the Juians were, but he attacked the swift creatures, severing limbs completely with the thick blade. An arm flew off to the left and its previous owner bounced right, squealing madly as blood sprayed from the wound. Then, flicking the blade again, Ezell eviscerated the beast in a spray of offal.

Ezell looked to the soldiers, ensuring he wouldn't be separated. The Ez fought hard, their blades spinning and flicking, though several were wounded. Adept as they were, the troop formed a ring, backing their panther's rears together to form a defensive circle.

Ezell kicked Boolen forward to join the ring, the circle tightening until each Ez had only enough space to swing his sword. The Juians tried to maintain their attack but hesitated, unable to break through the defensive barrier.

As the creatures chittered angrily amongst themselves—clear that they were unsure whether to attack or retreat—Ezell counted the troops. Three soldiers and two panthers lay dead. Ezell's pale blue eyes fixed on the torn bodies, flesh splattered across the ground. It made his stomach churn.

Two soldiers had died alongside their panthers, and though Ezell knew the great beasts were dead, he could see muscles still twitching within their gaping wounds.

He looked away to watch the Juians whose beady little eyes were watching the Ez soldiers.

Tense seconds passed before the Juians howled together and began to retreat. Taking the mauled corpses with them, they bounced off into the surrounding foliage. As they disappeared from view, Ezell released a sigh of relief and examined one of the dead Juians with disgust. Covered in black fur, their oversized teeth and savage grins were the first feature he noticed. Next was the upright thorax and abdomen, from which two sets of arms and a pair of legs sprouted. They were just as he had imagined from his studies, only more intimidating. They were nightmarish, with each of their six appendages ending in long, curved talons that were able to tear flesh from bone … he found himself suddenly thankful they were only found within the walls of the Western County, where only the bravest or most foolish Ez ever saw them.

Ezell knew there were few who'd seen a Juian in the flesh and fewer still who'd survived to tell the tale.

He grimaced. 'You fought well. You are a credit to yourselves, your training, and our fallen.'

The Royal Guards pounded their clenched fists across their armoured chests in salute.

'Is there anything we can do for them?' said one guard, pointing to the pools of blood that were all that remained of their fallen comrades.

'We can escape here and fight for the freedom of all Ez. They died knowing that they fought for—' Ezell closed his mouth abruptly as a noise reached his ears: the sound of something approaching fast.

'I heard it too,' whispered the most senior Royal Guard, Theon.

The undergrowth erupted as a black beast launched itself toward the surviving Ez. The Prince flicked up his sword to the ready but realised it wasn't the Juians; it was Edric.

'My Prince,' exhaled Captain Edric, as he brought his panther to a skidding halt before the ring of Royal Guards. Behind him, four more panthers and their riders dashed through the undergrowth to join him. 'We heard the clash of weapons and expected the worst. I came as fast as I could.'

Ezell wiped the blood off his sword and sheathed it. 'I thought the Juians favoured the forests south of here.'

'Normally, yes. The airship patrols must have stirred them up.'

Ezell nodded.

'They passed over us several times,' continued Captain Edric, 'but we managed to hide. It is easy—'

'To hear them coming,' Ezell finished Edric's sentence. 'We should keep moving.'

'Agreed. Especially if we're to have any chance of making it through the pass before the Humans block it.' He guided his panther to beside Ezell, and they both set off at a slow trot.

'Do you think they will block the pass?' asked Ezell, looking over his shoulder to see the rest of the soldiers falling into rank.

'I'm not sure. But if I were hunting fugitives who escaped into the Western County, that's what I would do.'

'I hope they don't think like you.'

'Plan for the worst and hope for the best, my Prince,' said the Captain. 'We can't afford to leave it to chance.'

'Have you heard from the other groups?' said Prince Ezell.

'The strength of this plan rested on separating into groups, so if one were caught, it wouldn't endanger the others. I left the rest of my group with those on the stream, and I haven't seen anyone else.'

'Have you heard from the forward scouts? Have they reached the pass?'

Edric shook his head. 'I don't have any more information, my Prince. We'll have to wait. It makes me wish Wilhelm was here. His abilities ...' Edric looked over his shoulder to make sure they couldn't be overheard, '... made him an excellent scout. We could really use his help right now.'

Ezell's brow furrowed as he remembered the events outside the dining hall in Ezguard. 'You weren't there, Edric. You didn't see what he did ...'

'You still haven't told me what happened,' Edric ventured.

'It was horrifying.' Ezell brushed his hand along his helmet as he reimagined the immense pain he had felt in that moment. 'His panther died.'

Silence stretched between them before Edric cleared his throat. 'There was always something strange about Zethish. Like she knew more than she should. Always watching people ... Did you notice?'

The Prince shook his head. 'I guess I was always worrying about other things.'

'Indeed,' said Edric. 'So, it started with Zethish dying ... ?'

As the ground beneath their panthers began to slope up toward the cliffs at the northern end of the Western County, Ezell told Captain Edric of the Governor's trap and how the Elven Healer turned his powers on the Humans. In quiet tones, he described how Wilhelm reacted to Zethish's death.

Edric's green eyes grew wide, still visible beneath his helmet. 'He just snapped?'

'They both did. One moment, the Elven Healer was treating Zethish, and the next, he pulled her blood into a big whip with his mancery.' Ezell's lip curled in disgust. 'And then the Humans retaliated and Wilhelm … Wilhelm just …'

'Just what?'

'He just stood there and screamed. I've never watched anyone experience pain like that before; even the Elves couldn't stop him.' Ezell stared into the distance, lost in the memory. 'He was so … powerful, and out of control. I agree we could use his scouting right now, but I think he's better off with the Elves.'

'Do you truly believe that?'

'I do, Edric. Only the Elves know how Truthseeing works. If there's anywhere Wilhelm needs to be, it's with them. They can teach him how to prevent his loss of control from happening again.'

'Do you think there are more like him?' said Edric, frowning at the Prince. 'Do you think there are more Ez Truthseers?'

'I don't know. I only just learned about Wilhelm. But if there were more, maybe Wilhelm could find them.'

'I thought the Elves were the only ones with those powers.'

'As far as we know,' Ezell shrugged.

'Then where do you think Wilhelm's powers came from?' the Captain pushed.

'I have no idea, but I want to know. Think of what we could achieve with our own Truthseeing.'

Edric absently scratched behind his panther's ears. 'The Elves left quickly,' he said.

'They didn't say much,' said Ezell. 'Just told me they needed to take Wilhelm for his own good, which I agreed to. I imagine they wanted to return and warn their Councils of the Humans' intentions.'

'Warn them they're at war again.'

The Prince nodded. 'But this time, it feels different.'

Edric made a concerned face. 'I would take you seriously if you'd been alive during the last war. Reading about it isn't the same as being there.'

'Oh, shove off, Edric, you weren't there either. I know you aren't *that* old. Besides, don't you think the Elves seemed genuine about helping us?'

Edric clicked his tongue in thought. 'Well, there's one thing for sure: if the Elves need our help, it must be bad news.' He locked eyes with Ezell. 'But I do agree. It does feel different this time. The Humans' arrival, the Elves, your father joining the Human Alliance and now Wilhelm's Truthseeing … I'm just not sure if it's all for the better.'

Silence fell a second time as Ezell pondered their discussion. Everything did feel interconnected in some way, but he couldn't understand why or how.

As the afternoon wore on and the rock walls loomed higher, Ezell allowed the Captain to take the lead, enjoying the comforting presence of his mentor. The sloped ground angled up towards the entrance of the Rift, the terrain changing as the undergrowth gave way to a goat trail that cut up through the craggy rocks.

As they finally topped the path onto the smooth stone at the Rift's entrance, Prince Ezell felt breath catch in his throat. It was like a huge fissure in the land, with walls of dark stone that seemed to sap what energy Ezell had left. The top of the cliff face was so tall that it looked to reach for the sky above them, and little light penetrated down to where they now stood.

'Have you ever been inside the Rift before?' said Prince Ezell.

'To my knowledge, none of the races have,' said Edric. The Captain's expression then became serious. Ezell grimaced, recognising his mentor's 'lecture face'.

'It is said that all life on Belissia started at the very top of our continent, in the aptly named Cradle of Life. The massive rock walls of the Cradle held the perfect conditions within to create and sustain a variety of life. In its fertile soil, and within those protective walls, life flourished for centuries. As time passed by, the predators grew larger and more vicious, forever in contest with the other carnivores for the finite supply of meat. Struggling to fuel their developing bodies, their appetites grew until they'd emptied the Cradle of all their prey. Then they turned on one another …'

Ezell rolled his eyes, but knew better than to interrupt the Captain.

'… carnivore on carnivore, beast on beast. Again, they evolved to gain the upper hand. Some became larger, and others shrank to hunt in packs, but no matter the change, neither could overcome the other. They drove themselves to the edge of extinction and needed to start exploring other places to survive. The unlucky ones found the Singing Pass, an eerily beautiful opening from the Cradle to the seas in the north. It is said they plummeted to their deaths in the thrashing ocean. And those that survived evolved to become the predators of the sea. But at the opposite end, the lucky few discovered a fissure. It led them right underneath the walls that had kept them trapped for all time, and through that rift they found a new world. Here on our fertile continent of Belissia, the predators were once again free to hunt.'

The Prince waited after Edric stopped before asking, 'Was that an answer?'

The Captain arched one eyebrow, like a father to his child. 'The panthers, Juians, Trolls, swamp raptors and whatever else lurks in the shadows of Belissia used the Rift to access Belissia from the Cradle. Though it formed an escape route, there may still be creatures within the Rift.'

'And you didn't think to tell me this before I decided to use it as our escape?'

'Well, we're here now,' said Edric. 'Besides, you should know all this. You studied the Old Religion as part of your classes.'

'I think I slept through most of them,' Ezell said, grinning mischievously.

The Captain shook his head in mock disbelief.

'What does the Old Religion say about us, Edric? Do we come from the Cradle as well?'

'No, the Old Gods fashioned us for this world and then protected us from the horrors of the Cradle. Which you would know, had you listened.'

'Edric, you know the Old Religion is falling from popularity, and its followers are dwindling. How can you justify the existence of the Old Gods when we've lived through centuries of Elven oppression?'

'I wouldn't begin to guess what the Old Gods intend for us.'

'If they do exist, their plan for us is a little twisted,' frowned the Prince, 'don't you think?'

Edric sighed. 'It's beside the point, my Prince. We aren't meant to know the divine plan. Why do you question the Old Religion so much?'

Ezell considered his response, 'If we really were created by omniscient beings, why wouldn't they support us or protect us against the Necromancer? And why would they allow the Elves to rule us for so long?'

'What if their place isn't to interfere but merely to create?'

'But why create us? For what purpose?' Ezell couldn't drop the point.

'When you find the Old Gods, you can ask them,' Edric smiled.

The sound of squabbling soldiers interrupted Ezell's answer, and he stopped to listen.

'See, there *is* more than one airship,' said the youngest of the Royal Guards, Mak.

Ezell turned Boolen from the Rift's entrance and gazed across the gargantuan bowl of the valley before him.

On his right, and to the west, soared the Border Ranges. The broad peaks jutted into the glow of the descending suns, and a wash of pinks and purples danced across the afternoon clouds. To his left, the Rift walls encompassed the valley and continued beyond sight to the south, the low escarpments still tall enough to keep most of the beasts contained within.

Draped between the cliff walls and the mountains lay the canopies of the Western County. Palettes of green were broken only by the bizarre mushroom trees, their towering trunks and pale, fleshy peaks. Ezell could see where the setting suns shone through the jagged tips of the Border Ranges, scattering rainbows of light across the mushroom trees' rubbery surfaces.

Ezell peered along Edric's outstretched arm and focused on the slow silhouette of a Human airship, raking the treetops with its downdraft. Unable to see any discernible details from this distance, Prince Ezell simply watched the ship's meandering course. He rolled his gaze further, scanning low to see another four ships circling in what the Prince guessed was an organised search pattern.

'I feel reasonably important if they've sent five airships after us,' said Edric. 'Looks like they thought we'd go south; they're heading towards Gavidgeon.'

'Hopefully, they'll stay there,' said Ezell.

'Hope for the best and plan for the worst,' countered the Captain again.

Ezell watched their silhouettes and found himself hoping that Edric was wrong about beasts lurking in the Rift. The Juians were scary enough, and they'd killed more of the soldiers than Ezell would have thought; let alone whatever might be lurking in the dark of the Rift.

Excusing himself, Edric called quiet orders to the Ez, sending several scouts back into the forest as guides for those still coming. With efficient forethought, the older Ez then arranged a handful of riders on the landing to protect against the chance they were followed on foot. His job done, Edric guided his panther next to Ezell.

'And now we wait,' he said.

Ezell nodded absentmindedly, distracted by his thoughts. They stood on the landing and faced the valley, following the criss-crossing patterns of the searching airships. Still hoping the ships would stay to the south, Ezell greeted the steady stream of soldiers that came up the path.

As the last rays of golden sunslight disappeared over the Border Ranges and the sky grew dark, the last of the Royal Guards padded onto the stone landing before the Rift. Bringing up the rear, the scouts confirmed they weren't followed, and with a quick count and a tick on his slate board, Edric nodded his head.

'All accounted for, my Prince,' he said, then his face dropped, 'except for the souls we lost to the Juians today and those still in Ezguard with the Humans.'

Ezell turned to the remaining Ez: 'We've out-manoeuvred them and given ourselves a head start. They have no idea where we've gone and won't guess where we're going, but they can be damned sure we'll be back. Let's use this lead and find our-selves a new base.'

The Royal Guards let out a collective grunt before saluting with their clenched fists pounding across their armoured breasts. In practised unison, they then arranged themselves into ranks and trot-ted into the Rift's entrance.

Bringing up the rear, Ezell paced Boolen beside the Captain and wondered if he would remember today fondly as the beginning of a new era, or would it become the beginning of the end?

Ezell sighed, hoping Wilhelm was receiving the care he needed in the hands of the Elves.

CHAPTER ELEVEN

'OF COURSE NOT,' said Grand Admiral Syn. 'He wanted nothing to do with Wilhelm.'

'But Neberadar, the Grand Librarian, did agree to train him?' Selouteau asked her father, as they strode along the marbled passages of Evenwood's underground. 'As head of the Truthseers, it is his duty.'

'He had no choice. I called a special session of the Councils and explained we needed to understand how the young Wilhelm had received his Truthseeing. They seemed rather concerned about the appearance of a Truthseeing Ez. Some of the Traditionalists even wanted to burn him by Pyromancer. Can you believe that? Thankfully, calmer heads prevailed, and they agreed to investigating and understanding Wilhelm.'

'Do you think there are more Ez like him?'

Syn's long strides remained even as he looked at her, his expression sincere. He was much taller than Selouteau, and his face was sharp and pointed: 'I admit I was surprised when you told me what happened in Ezguard, but I doubt very much this is an isolated incident.'

'So you think there are more?' Selouteau considered the implications. 'But where does their Truthseeing come from?'

'Where does ours come from?'

'From our blood,' she said automatically, 'just like our mancery. Every Elf knows that.'

'Maybe it doesn't. Maybe it comes from a source we don't understand.' He paused and let the weight of his remark sink in. 'I'm expecting Wilhelm will help us solve this little mystery, and I'm hoping the outcome will incite more cooperation between our races.'

'It's a little late for that, Dad. They've already joined the Human Alliance.'

'But the emergence of a Truthseeing Ez could alter the scales,' said Grand Admiral Syn.

'You're hoping there are more like Wilhelm, aren't you? You want to use them as soldiers.' She looked at her father. He had always been a calculating man, but Selouteau knew he had become colder since the death of her mother.

'Don't be so callous. I want to support and train them so they can fight for their own future. You know well enough the Ez population is as divided as the Elves. I have no doubt their King's treaty will provoke them far more than their Prince's exile.'

Selouteau realised her father had more agendas than she could count. 'Are you going to incite civil war amongst the Ez to win against the Humans?'

'War is a means to an end, not an outcome. What I want is to see the Ez freed from all oppression, including ours and the Humans. And I will do what needs to be done to see that happen. I would, however, very much like to know the terms of their agreement. I wager it heavily favours the Human Alliance.'

'How can it be any worse than two thousand years of tyranny?'

He looked at her unimpressed, but she met his cool gaze equally.

'Do you think the Humans came here for war?' said Selouteau.

'I find it hard to believe they travelled from wherever they hail for a few religious artefacts, Selouteau. I believe there are far more sinister motives at play.'

'Aren't there always?' she answered with a roll of her eyes. 'If there were religious artefacts here on Belissia, surely we Elves would already know about them.'

'You're incorrectly assuming the word "we" is a collective term for all Elves.' Syn made a careful observation of their surroundings. 'I've often found that King Eltavar and the Grand Librarian Neberadar operate in a league of their own, Selouteau, and the Councils as a whole aren't exactly known for their candour. There are things about the Necromancer's War … things that happened before I was elected to the office that they won't discuss, no matter how I ask the question.'

'What do you mean? And what would they gain by lying about the presence of another race's artefacts?'

'Time will tell, I'd surmise. Are you ready for your hearing?'

Selouteau grimaced as if in pain. 'Depends how long they take to decide my fate.'

'Don't be so flippant. That Truthseer's attitude is rubbing off on you, and it is very unbecoming. You should be far more serious about this.'

Stopping before a pair of great golden doors, the image of a tree spread across the timbered surface: the doors to the Council Chambers. Selouteau turned on her father and lowered her voice to a whisper. 'I would be far more serious if I knew exactly what was going on.'

'Selouteau—'

'No,' she cut him off, one long finger held up in warning. 'Against my own instincts, I played your puppet, did as you asked, and now we're on the brink of another war and I am being called before the Councils. What are you trying to achieve, Dad?' She looked into his eyes as if the Truth would reveal itself there. 'What do I say if they ask me to confess before a Truthseer?'

'You will have to tell the Truth, Selouteau. That's all I can ask of you.'

'The Truth would only condemn us both … I will have to lie to a Council and hope I am not caught.' She paused to glare before whirling away. Pushing through the golden portal, she stalked into the Council Chambers. They were empty, and with her boots echoing around the large circular amphitheatre, she took a moment to clear her mind.

The latest events at Ezguard notwithstanding, Selouteau had never broken protocol, nor had any Elf under her command. She'd performed her duties to the best of her abilities for as long as she could remember. Even the decisions she regretted—the ones that led to the deaths of her soldiers—she told herself they were for the good of the Elven race. Would the Councils count her one hundred years of service in her favour?

All through her career, Selouteau had been careful to analyse all outcomes and study each possibility before committing to any choice. That was why she excelled at what she did, because just like her father, she never stopped planning. Yet, she feared that her father's and now her decisions would be the start of the war with the Humans.

She wondered how the Elves had ruled for so long without a total revolution and why the Lesser Races hadn't organised a continent-wide rebellion after all this time. Was Prince Ezell right? Were the Lesser Races so scared of the Elven race that they would live under tyranny rather than fight for their freedom?

She sighed and was immediately conscious of the noise's amplification within the amphitheatre's reflective surfaces. She would not allow her actions to be the cause of a war. Instead, she focused on that dark surrounding stone and felt some of the tension slide from her shoulders. In its wake, she found herself hoping there were more like Wilhelm; more Truthseeing Ez waiting to be discovered.

Squaring her feet, Selouteau clenched her jaw, as the ancient timbers creaked with movement, as one of the Councils entered: this one was the Council of the Admirals of the Elven Armada. They were the highest-ranking military figures of Elven society. Each Elf proudly displayed a silvery uniform identical to that of Selouteau's, though with more awards spread across the breast.

At their head flowed Princess Dianella, Lady of Tanglewood, her supple frame impossible to miss even beneath the heavy golden robes. The Princess was the youngest of all the Council members and was, like Syn, elected into the power vacuum following the Necromancer's War. She was also one of the few Integrist supporters alongside her father. Here in this Council, she served as the Auditor: the one who presided over the meeting.

Next, her father, Grand Admiral Synnathril, Director of the Elven Armada, Prince of the Skies, Commander of the First Fleet and the only military commander ever given an accolade so high he was crowned royalty. To many, it was the single greatest honour any Elven Officer could hope for, but her father refused to explain what he had done to receive such distinction.

Selouteau had often wondered what feat he had achieved to gain his crown, surmising it must have been an amazing strategy or a victory against impossible odds during the Necromancer's War. But no matter how many times she asked, he would never tell. It was a constant source of intrigue for her and many other Elves.

She glanced at her father and frowned; his features were pulled tight across high cheekbones, a tell Selouteau knew conveyed his stress. She took both comfort and unease from his pained expression; happy he felt concerned about her fate, yet worried by his unease. Selouteau knew that if this Council asked her to confess before a Truthseer her career would be over, and her life.

And yet, Selouteau suddenly realised she agreed with her father. If there were more Ez like Wilhelm, they would need to be protected and trained to use their powers, whether the Councils agreed to it or not; they wouldn't agree, of course, because if the Ez held the power of Truthseeing and could read the minds of the Elves, then Elven reign over Belissia would crumble, as would any potential Human dominance. The Councils knew that if more Truthseeing Ez could be found and trained, the Lesser Races could defend themselves and earn the right to decide their own future. The Elven reign would end.

In a perfect world, the Elven leadership would allow the break from tradition and welcome the other races as equals with open arms. But with the current Traditionalist regime in power, Selouteau knew that would never happen. She hoped the Integrist movement could gain enough momentum to support such an ideal. Given enough time, they could. But time was something they did not have. The arrival of the Humans, the ensuing political mess and Wilhelm's burgeoning Truthseeing proved that change was occurring here and now.

As the Council of the Admirals of the Elven Armada moved to their seats, Selouteau acknowledged a shift in her thinking, one she hadn't thought was possible until recently. If there were more powered Ez to be discovered, Selouteau would protect them. Whatever the cost. Even if she had to operate without the Councils' approval, she would do so alongside her father.

A feeling of liberation spread through her as she realised it was the right thing to do. She wondered how many times her father had successfully moved behind the Councils' back, and how many operations he had approved without their consent, to do what he thought was right. She glanced curiously at the Grand Admiral, wondering again what he had done to earn his crown. It seemed ironic that an Elf so intent on working without Council knowledge would be crowned a royal and admitted to the highest of ranks.

She considered her next options. She would have to be careful, especially with who she could trust. Together with her father, she could plan for what was coming; they could map every possibility to ensure their decisions wouldn't lead to civil war. Or if war was to come, they needed to be ready and willing to do what was necessary to keep Wilhelm, and any other Truthseeing Ez, safe.

But a lingering thought turned her stomach cold. She couldn't shake the feeling she was following in Vylok's footsteps. She knew the Necromancer had taken action according to his beliefs and dragged Belissia into a war because of it. Was she any different?

Very little information on Vylok had survived the war, and truthfully, she knew nothing about him other than hearsay. No one did, because the Councils had removed all information about the Elf. Selouteau wondered what had provoked him to kill tens of thousands of Belissians. Was there one moment when everything changed and he chose to become a mass murderer? She wished she could research his history, but with such close-mouthed Councils, Selouteau doubted she would ever know the Truth. Whatever the case, she refused to believe she could ever condemn thousands of innocents to death.

'I call this session of this Council in session,' her father's voice echoed around the chamber.

Her back straightened, and she stood to attention. She clenched the muscles along her jaw. The last of the Admirals had climbed the tiered seating and now sat on the elaborately carved chairs, equally spaced around the upper and outermost ring of the amphitheatre.

The weight of their gazes fell on her, judging her every movement. Driving thoughts from her mind and willing her muscles to calm, her face became an impassive mask as she ran a smoothing hand down the front of her uniform.

'Captain Selouteau,' said another male voice.

Feeling confident, she replied, 'Yes.'

'Captain Selouteau,' boomed the voice again, 'do you know why you are here, standing before this Council of the Admirals of the Elven Armada?'

She turned to the speaker who stood now before his seat, unlike the other Council members. His chest puffed out beneath an immaculate Admiral's uniform of the brightest silver. An array of medals, pinned like a multi-coloured sash, weighed down his left breast.

Selouteau knew the Elf to be Admiral Kaan of Ibrasil, Commander of the Third Fleet. A bloodthirsty Traditionalist, his choice to wear every accolade he'd ever earned reflected his need to feel superior. She gazed into his predatory eyes, an unkind sneer working its way across his viper-like face. Rude, arrogant and self-indulgent, he never missed the opportunity to let others know he was gunning for the honour of Grand Admiral. He was every-thing her father wasn't and everything her father endeavoured not to be.

Kaan began his spiel again: 'Do you know why you are—'

'Yes.' She crisply cut him off with the single syllable.

His black eyes flashed, and even from this dis-tance, Selouteau could see the anger rising behind his dark features. He raised his finger pointedly at Selouteau and took a deep breath, but he was cut off again.

'Perhaps,' interceded Princess Dianella, her tone clear and bell-like, 'you should enlighten this Council as to why you are here, Captain Selouteau. And I would like to make note that your last visit was due to accolades for service in the Necromancer's War. You saved a great many lives that day.'

And killed many more, thought Selouteau.

'We all know how exemplary Captain Selouteau's career has been, but that is not why we are here,' snapped Admiral Gwydiir of Darkwood, Commander of the Fifth Fleet. He was the fattest Elf Selouteau had ever seen; his jowls wobbled as he spoke.

'Please, Captain Selouteau,' Princess Dianella said, opening her hands, 'regale us with how you came to stand before this Council.'

Selouteau bowed before the Elves and took a moment to breathe. She knew the only way she would get through the questioning and save her father was to lie. She knew what she was doing. She had thought about it, planned it and considered the risks. Knowing what Perch had told her about the Truthseeing not being foolproof, was perhaps the key she needed. But enacting it was something different … 'The Grand Admiral and I were contacted by Ezell, the Prince of the Ez.'

The eleven Council members shuffled on their chairs, exchanged confused glances and quietly cleared their throats. Gwydiir recovered first: 'This knowledge has not been made available to this Council, as neither you, Captain or the Grand Admiral have recorded your reports. How did the Prince of the Ez contact you?'

Her stomach grew cold, and a wash of regret coursed through her veins. Reality hit her: she'd just lied to some of the highest-ranking members of Elven society.

She took another breath to steady herself, and continued her lies. There was no other way …

'As I am sure you are all aware,' Selouteau replied, carefully remembering the story she had constructed, 'there are Ez located in every city throughout Belissia who operate as contacts for the leaders of the Lesser Races, should they need a direct conversation with an Elven representative. While conversing over Globcomm, the Grand Admiral and myself intercepted a plea for help from Prince

Ezell.' She watched the Council collectively turn to Syn, who stared steadily at his daughter, fighting to hide his surprise.

'The Prince requested our immediate help after revealing the King of the Ez was about to sign a treaty to join the Human Alliance, just like the Southern Islanders. Together,' she held her hand toward her father, 'the Grand Admiral and myself decided the quickest course of action would be to meet with the Prince and offer our guidance as he moved to stop the proceedings. Timing was critical; being closest to the Prince's location, I personally intervened. Unfortunately, Governor Thawn—who we have since learned is the highest-ranking Human official here in Belissia—was forewarned of the Prince's attack and signed the treaty the night before. Our situation escalated from a planned operation to a survival situation. We barely managed to escape, with the Prince and the Truthseeing Ez, Wilhelm.'

Admiral Kaan's beady eyes switched from Selouteau to Syn, gauging the situation between father and daughter. 'And you confirm this, Syn?'

Selouteau assessed her father as the skin pulled ever tighter across his prominent cheekbones. She recognised worry, stress and … admiration? His eyes twinkled as he turned to his rival. 'I do, esteemed Admiral Kaan.'

'I would like to remind this Council again that neither the Grand Admiral nor the Captain have submitted their reports,' continued Kaan.

'Considering both Elves in question were called into this session the second they landed in the capital, I find it hardly concerning they were unable to finish, let alone submit, their reports, Admiral,' said Princess Dianella.

'Captain Selouteau's crew members, however, did have the time to finish their reports; even one Lieutenant Wreadallanon, condemning his own actions against the Human Governor. Surely, you don't believe these ranking officers had no time to construct a report?' said Kaan, his rising annoyance evident.

The Council broke into a low murmur, each conversing to the Elf immediately adjacent and some seemingly talking to themselves. Selouteau kept her eyes low, not daring to meet any of their gazes as they whispered amongst themselves.

Every snort, comment and murmur became amplified by the dark, shining stone that surrounded them. She waited in the midst of her lies, allowing the wash of noise to flow over her, wondering if it would cleanse her guilty soul. She'd recited the lie as planned, but she had no idea how she would escape if they asked her to confess before a Truthseer.

'And are you willing to repeat your account before a Truthseer?'

She had no idea who had spoken, but immediately, Selouteau's stomach dropped. Her mind raced.

She would be discovered. Branded a traitor and convicted of treason, punishable by exile to the Cradle. Only one other Elf had ever received the exile punishment, but Vylok had avoided that through death.

Selouteau gulped, endeavouring to swallow the great lump that sat in her throat. She would become an exile, banished to the wilds within the Cradle. Locking eyes with her father, who had grown rigid in his seat, she nodded. There was no other choice: 'I am willing.'

CHAPTER TWELVE

ADMIRAL KAAN'S GRIN made him look like a swamp raptor. Without moving his beady eyes from Selouteau, he signalled to the great golden doors. 'Bring in the Truthseer.'

Again, Selouteau heard the timbers creak with movement and then fell back into place with a resounding boom. There were no footsteps, as she felt a presence approach her from behind.

'Truthseer, you were tasked to aid Captain Selouteau during her mission to Gusting and have since watched and ensured her actions adhere to this Council's mandate,' said Kaan.

Selouteau whipped her head around to see Perch standing beside her. She looked at him, her eyes searching his face, as thoughts raced around her mind. Perch's mind connected with her own, and immediately, she spoke across the link, *'You've been spying on me for the Councils, Perch?'*

'I'll explain everything, Captain, but for now, let's get through this hearing.'

To the people outside their link, Perch confirmed what Kaan had said, 'Yes, esteemed members of the Council of the Admirals of the Elven Armada. I have been with Captain Selouteau prior to Gusting and reported on her doings to the Councils ever since. As per my orders.'

Perch was a spy for the Councils! He'd been spying on her the entire time!

The skin on the back of Selouteau's neck crawled.

'Truthseer, we wish to know if Captain Selouteau has told us the Truth. It is of utmost importance that you inform us of any lies in her testimony.'

'Very well,' said Perch.

Selouteau's stomach turned cold.

Princess Dianella turned to Selouteau with a swish of her long hair. 'Please, Captain Selouteau, explain once more the events that brought you before us today.'

'Surround your thoughts in stone, Selouteau,' said Perch across their link, *'Just in case someone else is listening.'*

She felt his connection dissipate as she built a stone wall around her thoughts, just like the stone that surrounded them in the chamber. She pushed thoughts of Perch from her mind. She couldn't think about him and the fact that he'd been spying on her ... She had to tell the story again. And remember her lies.

When she finished recounting the story as she'd said it, Admiral Gwydiir called out, 'Truthseer, what did you find?'

'As true as my own recollection, and in corroboration with my Truthseeing, Captain Selouteau is recounting fact. This Council, and all Councils may take her account as accurate.'

It was a lie. The Truthseer was lying to the Councils, just like Selouteau had. Doing her best to control her face, Selouteau took a deep breath and swallowed past the lump in her throat.

Kaan stared at Selouteau, as Perch's words hung thick on the air. More than a few of the Council's faces reflected the surprise Selouteau felt. She struggled to keep her face a passive mask, lest the shock show on her face.

Emotions swirled within her. Fear and disappointment at Perch, and yet excitement at what he had done … what they had done. Struggling to clamp down on her thoughts, Selouteau noticed her father regarding them with an intrigued expression, while Admiral Kaan looked livid.

'That will be all. Thank you, Truthseer,' said Syn.

Perch didn't look at her as he turned to leave, but she did feel his mind brush her own, and he was … smiling. The doors creaked shut behind him, and the following silence weighed on Selouteau's conscience.

Everything had changed in that single moment. The future she had planned and worked so hard for disappeared as a new path opened—a path she would never have considered for herself. The path of an Elf who would break rules in the pursuit of what she thought was right.

Her desire to serve as a proud Captain of the Elven Armada had vanished, and she no longer felt the pressures of living up to her parents; one a Grand Admiral and one the deceased Great Inquisitor. She no longer felt the need to prove she was a worthy child of such legendary parents. Instead, she would follow her own path, one arguably harder—becoming an agent of change in Belissia.

The strangest sensation grew within her. As she stopped to consider it, she realised her muscles were tensed with excitement. Kaan's voice sliced through her thoughts. 'Do you know the punishment for treason, Captain Selouteau?'

Her stomach dropped as her eyes threw daggers at Kaan: 'Excuse me?'

Crimson flushed the Admiral's cheeks as he clambered to his feet. 'You heard me. The punishment for treason, do you know what it is?'

Her feeling of elation washed away, replaced with a chill that dragged at her innards. 'Exile.'

'Speak up,' he spat.

Selouteau fought to keep her own emotions in check. 'Treason is considered the highest criminal act and so is rewarded with capital punishment: exile.'

'No, Captain Selouteau, not only exile but complete banishment. If found guilty, you will be tossed into the Cradle forever.' His words echoed around the chamber.

Selouteau looked at the Council members, then at her father, whose face showed the same confusion she felt.

'I wasn't aware Captain Selouteau was under suspicion of treason,' said Syn.

'Come now.' Princess Dianella rose slowly from her chair at the head of the chamber. 'That is enough, Admiral Kaan. You have scared young Selouteau sufficiently. We all know we will not banish one of our best officers and most gifted mancers, particularly as we sit on the cusp of another war.' She turned her intelligent gaze on Selouteau. 'Captain Selouteau, we have no further questions regarding your actions particular to this event.'

'What?' stammered Admiral Kaan. 'She aided and abetted a now exiled Ez criminal—'

'Captain Selouteau acted as she thought fit after confirming her intent with her superior officer and a fellow Council member. Her actions have given us precious time to prepare ourselves for what is to come, now all confirmed by the Truthseer. You should be thanking her, Admiral, not chastising,' said her father.

Kaan continued: 'You will only invite further indiscretions from her, and others like her. This will only—'

'Sit down, Admiral,' bellowed Syn. 'The Truthseer's word is final.'

The Council members repeated Syn's words like a chant, 'The Truthseer's word is final.'

Kaan fell into his seat, but his furious eyes stared at Selouteau.

'Are there any further questions or comments for the Captain before we move to the next item?' said Princess Dianella. She waited until all members shook their heads before continuing: 'The fate of one Lieutenant Wreadallanon is still in debate, Captain. He attacked the highest-ranking official of a non-wartime race, disobeyed orders and acted out of revenge. Potentially, his actions could be the catalyst for the Humans declaring war.'

The Admirals all started talking over one another.

'For now,' said Grand Admiral Syn, in a tone that cut through the noise, 'the Lieutenant Wreadallanon will be remanded in custody, under the watchful eye of our soldiers. Until he can prove he is of sound mind, he will remain off the roster of active duty. I apologise, Captain, but you will have to find another Aquamancer to add to your crew for the time being.'

'Do we agree?' asked Princess Dianella, opening her hands to the Council members, who all nodded their heads and muttered affirmations. 'Excellent. We have nothing further for you—'

'If I may,' Grand Admiral Syn spoke over Princess Dianella, 'Captain Selouteau will need to remain within Evenwood for the foreseeable future while the Councils determine the best approach towards the Humans. In the meantime, Captain, finish your report and include any information the Humans may have revealed about the artefacts they seek. Perhaps these artefacts are important enough for us to perform our own search, especially if they're willing to go to war for them.'

'Have the Councils ever learned of such artefacts within Belissia?' said Selouteau.

'Not that I am aware of,' said her father.

'No,' confirmed Princess Dianella, 'not as far as this Council is concerned.'

Selouteau chanced a look at Admiral Kaan and noted his glance flicking between Dianella and Syn. She made a note to mention it to her father later, before saying, 'I have one last question before I go.' She waited for Princess Dianella's wave of approval. 'How is the young Ez, Wilhelm Torla of Gavidgeon?'

'Wilhelm has already begun preparations for his training. Neberadar, the Grand Librarian and Truthseer Supreme, will be sure to look after him.'

Relieved to know that Wilhelm would be trained to use his Truthseeing, she smiled and bowed deeply to the Council members before bidding her farewell.

Selouteau strode from the chamber unable to hide the smile that threatened to break her face in two. She had lied to the Councils with the help of a Truthseer. And she had gotten away with it. Her mind reeled at the possibilities of what that meant to not only her life, but the entire Elven regime, and all the races of Belissia.

The doors closed behind her and on the life she had once lived. And as she looked at all of the pathways ahead of her, Selouteau knew that speaking with Perch was the best place to start ... he had some explaining to do.

CHAPTER THIRTEEN

'I SHOULD BE going with you,' said Edric.

Ezell pulled away from his longscope and shook his head. They were standing on top of a sharp precipice that overlooked the city of Chancy in the Northern County.

'No, Edric. We both know that's not true. It took us ten days to travel up the Rift and then another two days to find a suitable set of caves. We're out of food, and the soldiers are uneasy. You must be the one to stay behind and keep them settled.'

'You should be the one to show them the way forward,' said Edric. 'They're here because of you, my Prince.'

Ezell gripped his panther's reins firmly and turned away from Edric to the view over the cliff edge.

'Let me go into Chancy and find this Defolt. While there, I can secure the supplies we need,' Edric continued.

'He'll only talk to me, Edric, and you know it. He's the Royal Contact, and I'm the royal.' Ezell glanced sideways at his Captain. 'We have to stick to the plan.'

'So you'll agree to being accompanied by two of the Guards?'

Ezell nodded, gazing outwards from his stance atop the sharp precipice. After escaping the Western County, they'd fled north via the Rift, racing up its narrow passages with all the speed their panthers would allow. On the ninth day of their getaway, glad to see a change from their monotony of the Rift, they'd reached an intersection in the fissure and branched east toward Chancy.

Knowing that the appearance of one hundred Royal Guards would be suspicious—even if his father hadn't already dispatched messengers to warn the Lords of the Ez—Ezell had led his men past Chancy. Using the dead of night to sneak through the ravine around the Ez city, they'd continued towards Lake Borlonn at the base of the Torre Falls. There, Edric had set up camp within a group of particularly well-hidden caves, in a dense patch of undergrowth.

From there—stomachs grumbling on half rations—Ezell and Edric had agreed for a small contingent to backtrack south and approach the Ez city of Chancy from the southeast, a far more believable direction to approach from. There, they'd followed the main road between Ezguard and Chancy to where they now stood, overlooking the Northern County's seat of power.

It was a beautiful city, and Ezell knew there were many who'd argue it *was* the most beautiful city in Belissia. White and pure, it sat in two halves on either side of a shallow, circular gorge that opened like an Islander prayer bowl over this section of the River Rift. Rising in steep terraces that cut into the sloping terrain, Chancy soared above the cold waters of the river in a majestic fashion.

Built from the dense white marble found in the Northern County, the rock was cut into tiles that clad every surface of the city, glittering in the rays of light from the twin suns. Rectangular towers and homes were stacked atop one another precariously, interconnected by steep roads and arching stone walkways. Looking down on the tightly packed buildings, Ezell found it hard to see where one ended and the other began.

Above each half of the city were the matching strongholds of Borlonn and Valerius, named after the brothers who had founded the city many millennia ago. Twin masses of the same white rock loomed high above the valley's rim on both sides and promised a rude welcome for any force foolish enough to attack the city.

Ezell shook his head, noting there was a good reason the Ez nicknamed Chancy the White City, because everything blazed white. He gazed over the Castle Borlonn on the opposite side of the valley, where the tightly packed streets climbed the hillside to rake at the base of its walls. The keep was an imposing fortress, dotted with countless windows and surrounded by a buttressing of smaller structures that seemed to hug the keep for support, as if cowering in its white magnificence.

Slender towers rose from the main fortress, but what held Ezell's attention was the massive glass window that dominated the southern wall of the keep. Overlooking the entire city, the River Rift and the surrounding valley, the window hid much of the keep behind its black, impenetrable facade, and although it brought a tinge of menace to the castle's image, Ezell knew its purpose was the exact opposite.

'I've heard Count Borlonn's audience chamber is behind that window,' said Edric.

'I've heard that too. Apparently, it reminds him of the wide-ranging effects his decisions have on his charges. It ensures he always does the right thing for everyone.'

Edric scoffed. 'No matter what you do or how noble your intentions, you're always going to piss someone off.'

Ezell raised an eyebrow and looked sideways at the Captain. 'You really aren't helping my state of mind.'

Edric slapped the Prince playfully on his unarmoured shoulder. 'Everything will turn out as it's supposed to. Have a little faith, my Prince.'

'Faith? When all this is over and the Ez are in charge of their own destiny, then I will think about faith. Until then, we will continue to hope for the best and plan for the worst; a great mentor once told me that,' said Prince Ezell.

'Indeed,' chuckled Edric.

'Look after yourself and the soldiers, Edric,' said Ezell with a nod of his blond head.

The Captain inhaled, his muscular shoulders filling his armour before he spoke. 'You know I will. For now, though, you need to worry about getting in and out of Chancy without anyone recognising you. That is of more concern to me.'

Ezell nodded and motioned for the other soldiers to step forward. 'I hope word of our escape hasn't reached Count Borlonn. If he hears either of us are in the city ...'

'He will have troops everywhere,' said Edric, as he swung himself up into the saddle. 'I'll give you a few hours before the troops and I head in to buy our supplies.'

'And I'll concentrate on winning over Defolt,' the Prince replied.

With a cluck of his tongue and a tug on the reins, Edric turned his panther. 'Happy hunting, my Prince.'

'You too, Captain,' said Ezell.

He watched his friend and mentor spur his panther to a trot, before looking down at the road leading to Chancy. The Ez of the Northern County had built a zigzagging cobblestone road that twisted down the cliff walls, past the Castle Valerius and through a watch house, where it then connected with the tightly packed streets of the city. Ezell could already feel the rawness on his heels that would soon turn into blisters. But he knew what had to happen. Taking the first step, he moved away from the cliff edge and started walking down the sloping cobblestones.

The soldiers followed, and they made frustratingly slow progress as they picked their way down the slippery cobblestones.

'It would have been much quicker if we took our mounts,' mumbled Mak, the youngest.

'You know exactly why we can't. We'd draw too much attention. On foot and dressed like this,' Theon tugged at the rags the three of them wore as disguises, 'we look like commoners so we can slip in and out without a problem.'

'We're Royal Guards,' protested Mak. 'We shouldn't have to walk, ever ...' Ezell turned to watch the young soldier wrinkle his nose at the clothes they were wearing. '... or dress like this.'

Theon tried to shush Mak and dropped his voice to a whisper. 'Think of how the Prince feels.'

Ezell smiled. Years spent in the courts of Ez nobles meant he'd trained his ears to hear even the quietest of uttered words. His father had always said that listening was a useful skill when secrets were power.

'I wouldn't be doing this either if I didn't have to. Do you think I'd dress like this out of amusement?' said Ezell.

The two soldiers sniggered. Ezell knew he looked ridiculous. With limited props and dwindling time, his soldiers had done their best to turn the Prince into a person who resembled a commoner.

They'd managed to hide most of his muscular frame beneath a simple saddle blanket, stitched with squares of other fabric swatches. Intended to look like a poor man's poncho, the light musky scent of panther sweat on the material only added to his disguise. They'd cut a hole from the cloth that doubled as a silly-looking hat, under which his blond hair—usually immaculately clean—was so marred with dirt it looked several shades darker. His face was also smeared with streaks of mud.

Based on what he remembered of the people of Chancy, Ezell knew they should have no problems sneaking in and out of the city unrecognised; the Chancians wouldn't look past their own pompous noses to recognise the dirty Prince passing through their city. And if his disguise was as revolting as it felt, then it must be convincing.

While Ezell had never travelled to the White City before, he had met many Chancians in his father's court in Ezguard. Ezell had found them to be self-important, self-interested and aloof. As the Prince of the Ez, he was forever being found and spoken to by the most outspoken of Count Borlonn's cult-like followers. He'd been a target for so many of their idealistic speeches about pacifism that he'd lost count.

Ezell knew that their notion of pacifism and that violence was unjustifiable was a worthwhile concept and had told them as much time and time again. But what he couldn't agree with—and what they failed to see—was that Ezell had been taught that conflict was not inherently evil. Ezell's teachers had instructed that conflict, if used appropriately, could be utilised to bring about resolution.

Never could he support violence as the entire means of resolution, nor could he support pacifism as an answer by simply avoiding conflict. As far as Ezell had been taught, everything had a time and a place. And although he'd tried to explain as much to the Chancians, they'd never listened, so every time, they ended in an arguement.

Turning around another switchback, Ezell ran his hand along the stacked stones that made up the small wall next to the cobbled road.

'My Prince,' came a voice from behind.

Ezell turned his head toward Mak, who along with Wilhelm was one of the youngest soldiers awarded the privilege of serving the crown as a Royal Guard and was only a few years younger than Ezell. 'Yes?'

'Do you think we will ever get to go home?'

'Why would you ask that?' said Ezell, stopping to lean against the low brick wall.

The young Ez stammered and looked away from Ezell. 'I … It's just … Well, you see, there's this girl I like back in Ezguard, and some of the guards were talking, saying they wondered if we'd done the right thing. I … I just hope to see Keera again,' said Mak, obviously blushing despite the layers of mud on his young face.

Ezell watched the boyish soldier look away, clearly embarrassed. Since they'd fled the caves in the Western County, Ezell had pondered that very same question. It haunted him, demanding an answer he couldn't find. And the harder he pushed, the more elusive it seemed.

At the time, it had felt right, and even now, Ezell knew he'd make the same decision again. The Ez could no longer live under the rule of another race, and it was well past the time they should have reclaimed their independence from Elven oppression. He and his father agreed on that but disagreed on how.

He looked at the soldiers shooting nervous glances his way as they awaited his answer. 'We all made our choices, and we're going to have to live with them. I believe it is time for the Ez to rule their own future, and the Humans are not the answer. I wouldn't change what I've done. I can't tell you if I made the right choice, and I cannot tell you if you will ever see Keera again.

'I cannot stand by and watch our people join an Alliance we know nothing about. For all we know, they could be more tyrannical than the Elves. I admit this is not how I thought things would transpire, but I stand by my decision.' Ezell regarded them in turn, meeting each of their gazes with a fierce determination. 'Both of you and the rest of the Guards need to make up your own minds. For one reason or another, you decided to follow me into exile. Why was that?'

Theon cleared his throat and spoke slowly, as if still piecing his thoughts together. 'I agree with you, my Prince. The Humans appear as secretive and untrustworthy as the Elves. I believe we can make a difference by taking a stand.'

Ezell smiled at the older guard. 'We already made a difference, because if there are this many soldiers amongst the Royal Guards who believe as we do, surely there must be many more Ez out there. Soldiers, fathers, women and children, all waiting for the chance to rally behind a future they can believe in. We need to give them that chance.'

Ezell then turned his pale blue eyes on the younger soldier. 'Why did you join me in exile, Mak? Why step away from a career full of respect and admiration, and from Keera?'

'I'm not really sure why I followed you.' Mak looked down, his brow scrunched in thought.

Ezell studied the smaller Ez's face; he was barely a man. 'Deep down, I'm sure you know why you're here.'

Still not looking at Ezell, the younger Ez nodded. 'It's silly. I thought it would be like the fairy tales, full of brave Princes with treasure and daring adventures. I wanted a story to tell Keera and maybe get enough gold so that she would ...'

Ezell burst into laughter and said, 'I can promise you it will be an adventure. Though I'm not sure about enough gold to impress Keera.'

Smiling bashfully, Mak continued. 'Do you plan to take the throne?'

Ezell's smile waned. His face dropped. To his left, Theon's features darkened, and he muttered something under his breath. The young guard did not know the line he'd crossed: for Ezell to take the throne, he'd have to kill his own father.

The Prince looked at Theon, who shied away, not meeting his eyes. 'Is that what the soldiers are saying?'

Mak nodded. 'They're saying it could be a civil war.'

Theon shot the young soldier a look that dripped in venom.

The Prince took a breath. 'So, some think I'm a usurping, power-hungry prince ... My father is the rightful ruler of the Ez, and I am the rightful heir. I have no desire to forcefully remove my father from the throne, but I will, with all my power, oppose his decision to join the Human Alliance. I am hopeful that others will join us as well. With enough support from the nobles and the general population, we could change my father's mind,' said Ezell, careful to not divulge his plan to work with the Elves to his men just yet.

'You didn't say if it would lead to civil war or not?'

Ezell grimaced. He could feel the weight of leadership hanging over his head. 'You're a lot smarter than your age, Mak, and one day, you'll make an exemplary officer ... I will not push the Ez into a civil war to make my point. I have no desire to see Ez fighting Ez.'

'So you're a pacifist? Is that why we're here in Chancy?'

'Not quite. I'm here in the hope of finding allies to support our cause.' He tried his best not to lie without revealing the Truth. 'I'm hoping we will find others here who believe it's time the Ez were their own people. Does that answer your questions and the whisperings of the soldiers?'

Mak nodded slowly, the concentration on his face telling Ezell he would think carefully about what had been said.

Ezell smiled, but it faded from his face as he turned to continue down the cobbled road. He knew he hadn't answered the question, but the exchange had helped clarify his own thoughts. He felt better knowing he would make the same decision again, even with the power of hindsight. Though the fact that the soldiers were whispering behind his back troubled him.

Ezell spared a thought for the upcoming meeting with Dane Defolt. He wondered how it would play out and shook his head with cynicism. The possibilities were endless, and if the last few weeks were anything to judge by, Ezell knew that anything might happen.

Chapter Fourteen

THE DESCENT INTO Chancy led them beneath the looming fortifications of Castle Valerius, with its gatehouse straddling the road ahead. In the shadow of the massive white fortress, the gatehouse looked tiny, but Ezell knew better. It wasn't designed to fend off a full assault but merely slow them down and create a choke point where any attackers would be open to attack by the twin castles.

He glanced up to the Castle Borlonn on the opposite ridge and could see the protruding noses of catapults sticking out over the battlements.

A Guard of Chancy, identifiable by the white castle crest emblazoned across the breast of his armour, stepped from behind the gatehouse's open portcullis and out onto the cobblestones. Holding a halberd in one hand, he held up the other and spoke in a gravelly voice. 'Halt.'

Ezell pulled his face into the best vision of a downcast traveller he could muster and eyed the soldier's long sword with envy. As part of their disguise, Ezell and his Guards chose to carry only small knives, knowing their usual hand-and-a-half swords would draw unwanted attention.

The Guard of Chancy stood still as a statue with his gauntleted hand held before him. 'You are entering the city of Chancy, capital of the Northern County and home to the Honourable Count Borlonn. State your business.'

Ezell stopped several paces from the Guard of Chancy and watched the soldier look them over, distaste clearly evident in the twist of his lips. 'Please, sir, we are but weary travellers seeking refuge and a warm meal.'

'We do not allow beggars inside the walls. Have you coin to pay for the services?'

Ezell brought out and jingled a large pouch of coins, it was tightly bound and had been hidden beneath a fold in his muddy poncho, 'Begging your pardon, sir, the road is long and leaves us looking less than ideal for our visit to the White City.'

'You don't sound like commoners,' the guard said, wariness entering his pale green eyes, 'and that's a lot of coin. What is the nature of your visit?'

'We are merchant agents from Silverton, searching for the finest Ez goods so that our Lord, Baron Delmai, may sell them to our newest neighbours, the Humans. We want to be sure they get only the finest of goods.'

The Guard stiffened, and his fingers tightened on the haft of his weapon. 'Baron Delmai is a Grain

Baron from the Southern County, his castle and lands are to the south of Granville.'

'Of course,' said Ezell, nodding calmly, as he continued the lie. 'The Baron is eager to get out of farming and is stretching into other ventures. He hopes to find lucrative business in selling the finest delicacies to the Humans. We know the Chancian wines, cheeses and pastries are known to be the best. We are here to sample and choose our wares and make contracts with suppliers and wagoneers for delivery to Silverton.'

'Then why are you dressed like that?' said the guard, pointing to their muddied ponchos. 'No merchant of Chancy would deal with someone who looks like a pauper.'

The Prince paused, realising either their disguises were too good, or the guard too smart. 'It is planned as such: who would try to rob three poor travellers? We plan to purchase better attire before we visit the merchant houses.'

The Guard of Chancy relaxed visibly as he looked at each of the three in turn. 'You should try the cider.'

'Cider?' said Ezell.

'It is a light wine, mixed with a sparkling mineral water found in the mountains to the north of here. Delicious, sweet and deadly.'

Confused, Ezell looked at Theon and Mak, who shook their heads. 'How do you mean "deadly"?' he asked.

Armour clanking, the guard moved to sit on a small seat at the base of the gatehouse, pushed against the white stone of the fortifications where he couldn't be seen by anyone coming down the hill. He settled himself and chuckled. 'It is the latest frivolity here in Chancy. Half the city is drunk on it at any one time. I had some last night and barely remember getting home. I say deadly, because it sneaks up on you and kicks like a mule.'

Typical Chancians. Ezell struggled to stop himself rolling his eyes in disgust. 'Sounds like a treat. We'll be sure to try it while we're here.'

The Guard waved them through the gate with a lazy move of his hand. 'Try the White Stallion. It's a tavern on the southern side of the city in the lower levels on Marble Street. Arguably the best cider in the Northern County. It also has rooms for rent and hot baths, and the food isn't bad either. Oh, and if you're looking for clothes, try Ellary on Cobble Lane.'

'Many thanks, sir.' Ezell waved over his shoulder as they continued past the gatehouse and into the twisting, near vertical streets of Chancy. He led them as close to a direct path towards the river as he could, choosing the steepest, most dangerous-looking streets in the hope that they would speed their passage and hopefully get out of their clothes.

All around him, the white walls of Chancy's buildings rose vertical, directing all the traffic into the tightly packed streets, though Ezell decided the term 'street' was inaccurate. Gloomy despite their brightness, they were more akin to alleyways; tight, serpentine passages that angled sharply through the white-washed city. It left Ezell wondering how any wagons would be moved through the streets.

He stumbled slightly and looked down to see that even the cobblestones were a pale white. Ezell shook his head, wondering how bright the city would be in the peak of the twin suns' rays.

They reached an intersection, and Ezell checked for traffic before they continued downward. The older of the two soldiers spoke, 'He was a breeze once he realised we had money.'

Careful to keep his voice low in case they were being followed, Ezell said, 'It's all they care about in the Northern County. How deep your pockets are, and how much food and wine you can stuff into your gullet.'

'Not a bad way to live in an uncertain world,' Theon replied.

'It's an ignorant way to live,' Ezell said, as he stepped around a group of young men, all roaring with laughter. 'They remain disconnected from the rest of the Ez.'

'True, and their position in the Northern County doesn't help.'

The Prince frowned in thought as he crossed another intersection and skirted around a trio of female Chancians, all of whom turned their noses up at him. 'What do you mean?'

'Chancy is the most northwestern of all the Ez cities. It's isolated by terrain on nearly all sides; the

Rift to the west, the Cradle to the north, Lake and River Borlonn and the Silver Lake to the east.' Theon gestured in each direction as he spoke. 'The only true passage into the White City is from the south, either by the ferry services on the Silver Lake or by travelling across the Blue Plains from Ezguard. Either way, the city is only approachable from the south.'

'What are you saying?'

Theon leaned in close and muttered, 'My Prince, I'm merely saying that their self-important attitude may be born from their geographical location, because they are so isolated.'

'That's not an excuse. They're quite content to rave about pacifism to the rest of the realm without stopping to examine what's happening around them. They don't even try to understand,' said Ezell.

'I'm beginning to think you don't like them,' Theon replied, one eyebrow raised.

'Not really, but unfortunately, that is the nature of working with a court,' said Ezell.

'So if you don't like them, why are we here looking for allies?'

The street in front of them ended in an abrupt intersection. To their left, the white cobblestones rose back up the hillside, and to the right, they fell sharply away. Moving so he could keep one hand on the wall in case of slipping, Ezell turned down the hill and said, 'Our options were limited, and Chancy is our best option to escape the Human Governor. You saw how many airships they sent after us.'

'With all due respect, my Prince ...' Theon looked around to ensure no one was within ear shot before he continued, '... I was wondering if you had something a little more solid in mind. I'm a scout for the Royal Guards and a cartographer—well, I used to be, anyway. It was my job to survey and plot the Belissian landscape, and although I agree our best escape from the Western County was the Rift, I'm a little concerned we're cornered up here. There are not many escape routes from Chancy.'

'In Ezguard, under my father's rule, soldiers— even Royal Guards such as yourselves—would never have spoken to a noble like that,' said Ezell. He stopped to face them, a broad, white-toothed smile stretching across his grimy face. 'I like it. It tells me there is a change on the horizon, and that is some- thing we all want and need. It's why we are here.'

As the two Guards gave each other blank looks, Ezell continued. 'I cannot tell you anything more. Not yet, anyway. Not until I have made contact. But trust that I have a plan in mind and that I wouldn't have led us into this without thinking it through.'

Theon nodded, but Ezell felt it was a noncom- mittal gesture, one intended to diffuse the situation more than to convey the scout's agreement. Ezell knew some of the older soldiers had reservations about his age and his ability to lead the troops. Ezell would let it slide for now. His actions would prove them wrong.

They continued toward Chancy's lower lev- els, where the smell of fresh water and cool air reached Ezell's nose. As they turned down another busy street, more disgusted looks were thrown their way, and ahead of them, Ezell saw the sign for the White Stallion. It was an ornate sign, a yard wide and emblazoned with a rearing stallion. The gaudy display hung above a set of polished double doors inlaid with an intricate weave of crafted metalwork.

Mak's face revealed his scepticism as he considered the single storey dwelling before them. 'I thought it was a tavern, a bath house and an inn, but it doesn't look like much from here.'

Ezell strolled forward and opened the entrance. 'The Chancian buildings are built in reverse to Ezguard's. We're entering on the top floor. The rest of the White Stallion is below us, down the valley wall.' He caught the briefest look of surprise flickering across the young Ez's face as he pushed through the doors and into the room beyond.

Although the White Stallion's top floor tried to convey a sense of wealth, Ezell had grown up within the Royal Palace, and to him, the tavern looked tacky. The stone walls were covered with a multitude of russet timber planks, all polished to bring a sense of warmth to the cold, white stone. Lanterns were spread around to reinforce the soft light, and little pots of burning herbs lent a spicy scent to the air. Ezell was sure some Chancians thought it exotic. A large, dangling chandelier made from the severed antlers of innumerable Blue Deer hung high from the ceiling. Tables set at a comfortable distance from one another sported an assortment of clientele—some drinking in loud, obnoxious tones, and some whispering deals in hushed voices. To his left, a barman stood behind the large russet timber bar, and to his right an empty desk.

Ezell descended the few stairs from the entrance's landing to the floor of the tavern, as beside him, Mak walked with his mouth agape. Across the room for all the customers to see was a wide opening that allowed the patrons to walk from inside to the outside with ease. And it gave an unending view of the full grandeur of Chancy's northern slope, glistening in the blinding sunslight. Mak stood stunned into silence by the sheer beauty of the White City scaling the north wall of the valley. It glittered and twinkled in the morning's daylight that bounced off the many surfaces in unimaginable ways.

'Whoa!' said Mak, his mouth still open.

'Despite what you said about these people, my Prince, I could get used to living here,' said Theon.

Ezell whirled on him, eyes flashing. 'My name is El.'

Theon's face turned red with a fierce blush. 'Sorry, El.'

Ezell cast a quick glance around, ensuring no one had heard his muttered name. 'Go and find us a room and take a bath.' He placed a hand on Mak's shoulder as the youth turned to leave, eyes wide and grinning at the mention of a bath. 'But nothing overstated. Choose something on the bottom end of average; we don't want to draw too much attention.'

'And what are you going to do, El?' Theon's voice dropped to an almost inaudible murmur. 'We're meant to protect you.'

'I have some business here first. I will join you later.'

Theon shot him a questioningly look, and Ezell returned it, willing Theon to read his thoughts. 'I'm enjoying the mud for now … I'm not ready for my face to be seen.'

Theon nodded in understanding and headed to the patron desk.

Ezell watched them go. It had been more nearly two weeks since their flight from the caves, and before that, they'd spent almost two weeks underground. Though the streams in the Western County were clear and adequate for bathing, they were nothing compared to the hot, regular baths that were commonplace within Ezguard.

Knowing mere hours separated him from scrubbing the mud, sweat and stress from his tired body, Ezell motioned to the barmaid and settled himself at a table in the corner of the tavern. Sinking onto the timber chair, which creaked in protest, he rolled his neck and eyed the surrounds.

Two score Ez hovered around the room in various states of sitting, standing, laughing or sleeping. He scrutinized all of them, and in the long moments before the barmaid finished serving meals to a table on the far side of the room, Ezell was certain none of them were the contact he sought.

Though he had never needed to make use of a royal contact before, Ezell knew the procedure. It had been drilled into his memory by his teachers over countless hours, often at unexpected times of the night. They'd ensured that if he was ever abducted or lost, he could replicate the task and call help silently to his aid. He wondered if that would be the case today.

The barmaid finished serving the steaming meals and turned to smile alluringly in his direction, her hazel eyes flashing as she flicked her long red hair. The pretty girl approached, her fleshy bosoms pale and bursting from the bust of her tightly woven corset. He stopped himself from rolling his eyes at such calculated use of the female body and wondered if the idea was hers or a requirement of her employment. He watched the rest of the tavern's patrons, hungry eyes following her shapely curves bounce with every movement. Whichever was the case, it was obvious that it worked.

'What can I getcha ... honey.' She struggled to finish her sentence, nose wrinkling at his stench.

'Sorry,' he said apologetically, 'I've been on the road for more than a week, and while I need a bath, I have a vast longing for a beer and hearty meal.'

'Oh honey, not to worry. I was just surprised. I'll have you sorted out back in two shakes of a cat's tail. You talk real pretty for someone dressed like a beggar.'

He held her gaze warmly, wondering if she thought anything was amiss. 'I am a merchant from Silverton. I'm afraid I don't always look this travelworn.'

She laughed lightly, a noise Ezell knew she'd trained to melt the toughest of Ez. She leaned forward, showing her ample cleavage. 'We don't get many from near the Ez capital up this way. The southerners seem to disagree with our way of life.'

'I'm just here to buy wares, not to judge.' A lie. He'd done nothing but judge the Chancians since he'd arrived. He waited as her eyes roved over the folds of his makeshift poncho before she made eye contact with him. 'I'll have one of the house specials and a small beer,' said Ezell.

'The cider is very popular at the—'

'Just the small beer to wash it down, please.' He kept his voice crisp but not rude.

'Of course, honey,' she winked, swishing her hips from side to side as she disappeared into the kitchen.

Ezell watched her go. Her guiles wouldn't work on him—he wasn't interested in women—but her behaviour had settled his decision. Clearly, she chose to dress and act like that, and he wouldn't be surprised if she sold information. Not strictly illegal, it was certainly frowned upon and mostly occurred when rival merchant guilds entered a period of economic disagreement. Ezell knew they paid handsomely for any information that would allow them a competitive advantage, and here, with drunk patrons aplenty, she could make a small fortune on the side.

He wondered how those guilds settled their disputes in a county where fighting was illegal. Musing, he turned his speculative gaze on the view shining through the broad space, open to the Chancian air.

Pondering the northern Ez and keeping a watchful eye on those around him, Ezell waited for his meal. Within minutes, the pretty maid returned. Clearly unconvinced that she couldn't win him over, she placed his meal and drink on the table before him, bending so her cleavage waved in his face. 'Are you sure there isn't anything else I can get for you, honey?'

Ezell shook his head. 'Thank you, that will be all for now.'

The barmaid winked in turn and dropped her voice low. 'I'll see you later then, honey.'

Ezell watched her swish away, heat colouring his cheeks. He wasn't interested, but he also wasn't use to such a public display of intimacy. In an effort to distract himself, he busied his hands with the arrangement of his meal. His hungry eyes roved the steaming plate, piled high with mashed potatoes, sausages and boiled vegetables smothered with gravy. The piping hot food called to him, his stomach screaming at his hands to pile mouthfuls onto the fork and force it down his throat.

Over the past two days and on limited supplies, he and his soldiers had lived on half rations. While they wouldn't die from starvation, the presence of a well-cooked meal sitting before him, especially one he couldn't eat, was torture. Clenching his fists, he stared at the meal and wondered why he hadn't thought to order two plates. He relaxed his whitened knuckles and promised himself he would buy another meal. This one, annoyingly, he needed as a signal to his contact.

Ezell moved the plate to sit on the edge of the table, next to his right hand. He placed the utensils together and across the top, prongs and blade pointed at his chest. He then pushed the tankard of beer to his left hand and turned the handle to face the door. Then, sitting back in his chair, he waited.

CHAPTER FIFTEEN

WILHELM SANK INTO the thick leather cushions of the couch and stared at the lavishly furnished quarters around him: a second couch across from him, a thick grey rug and a squat table covered in books and scattered papers all written in the Elven language that he couldn't read.

He picked up a ring from the small table before him and turned it over in his hands. Though he looked at the small piece of jewellery, he wasn't really interested. He felt as if nothing could interest him. Not without Zethish.

He looked at the blue gem grasped within a simple golden band, and rolling the small ring between his fingers, he noticed a growing feeling of warmth seep through his fingers and hands. As the sensation spread up his arm, Wilhelm noted his mood grew the barest shade lighter.

He waited in the silence, feeling empty and hollow. Zethish was dead. His best friend gone forever, taken from him by the Humans. And though that Elf hadn't killed her, he had used his sorcery to drain her blood to make a weapon. Wilhelm choked on a fresh wave of tears.

More than anything, Wilhelm wished she were here. She always knew what to say and how to cheer him up. She was clever like that, always ready to help him when he needed it the most.

When Wilhelm's father had forced him to join the Royal Guards, he'd been told to choose his panther as the beast he would ride for the rest of his life. But she chose him. From across the nursery, she had looked at him with her intelligent green eyes from within the mass of playing cubs. There, silent and still, she called to him by name as her mind reached out to his own.

From the very beginning, she'd been different from the other panthers, whispering that no other panther could talk to his mind. And she'd proved it, for when she'd urged him to contact other panthers with his Truthseeing, none of them understood.

Tears rolled from his eyes.

They had been best friends. Inseparable. The best in every class at the King's College for Royal Guards. They were a team, a force to be reckoned with—their combined intelligence, speed and strength—ensuring nothing stood in their way.

Together, they'd graduated the top of every class and were assigned a coveted position among the Prince's closest guards. Even though Prince Ezell had learned of Wilhelm's capabilities, Zethish had made him promise to never tell anyone else; she had remained his greatest secret.

It was Zethish who had encouraged him to approach the Prince about exile. She was the one who first noticed the Prince's motives and urged Wilhelm to seek allies amongst the ranks of Royal Guards. She'd again helped him then, showing him how easily he could see into the minds of others and judge when they were lying—just like the feared Elven Truthseers. She had even shown him how to hide his mind when the Truthseers were nearby. But even that felt like nothing without her. He suddenly wished she had never told him to confront the Prince and help Ezell defy their King. Because without the Prince's political exile, Zethish would not have been killed.

Wilhelm sobbed as the image of her broken body came to mind. Her matted fur, difficult breathing and blood leaking across the polished floor. And the pain. Through their link, Wilhelm had felt every bolt of energy break through her skin. Every burning shot melting flesh and muscle as if it were his own. Worst, the confusion and fear in the moments before death. Linked with her, Wilhelm had tried to comfort her passing, but she took that journey without him. By then, she was only a soulless body taking its last, dying breath, and like that, she'd simply vanished.

He knew there were other things he should be caring about. He knew the Elves had never accepted an Ez aboard one of their beautiful airships, nor had they ever let outsiders into their city. It should have been a momentous occasion, marking the beginning of a new era with the Elves displaying a separation from their Traditionalist values. But it wasn't. Instead, he'd spent the journey in silence. In fact, he couldn't remember a single moment of the journey. Not the airship, nor the air docks, nor the walk through the fabled City of Trees, Evenwood. Not even how he came to be in this underground chamber. All he remembered was his heartbreaking solitude.

A memory of the Elf Captain, Selouteau—her strong face and incredible height—flashed into his mind; she'd apologised for the way they'd knocked him unconscious and dragged him from Ezguard … not that he remembered. Wilhelm rolled the ring around in his fingers, as he let the memory develop in his mind until another mind sliced into his thoughts like a knife.

'*Tell me how you got these powers,*' said a powerful male voice that sent lances of pain through Wilhelm's thoughts. '*When did you first notice you could see the Truth in others' minds?*'

Wilhelm looked up at the intimidating figure, who was even taller than Captain Selouteau. Wilhelm shoved his hands beneath his legs on the cushioned seat—like he'd done as a boy when his father yelled at him—and wondered how long the Elf had been standing there.

The towering Elf had a sharp beak of a nose. His silvery white hair gleamed in the dim lighting, and his thin shoulders were set with a regal air. Wilhelm looked into the Elf's hard eyes and sensed the movements of a dark and malicious mind behind them. Wilhelm could tell in that instant that the Elf didn't want him there.

A consciousness so powerful it obliterated everything but its presence bore down on Wilhelm. He gasped as the Elf's Truthseeing forced its way into his thoughts—like a blade piercing his skull—and began probing Wilhelm's deepest memories.

'*Where do your powers come from, young Ez?*' said the Elf. '*Who passed it on to you? Your mother or father?*'

Wilhelm tried to respond, but his words were silenced by a force that could have moved mountains.

'*There's no need to answer. I will find the Truth.*'

Frozen in place by the Truthseeing, Wilhelm sat clenching his hands, feeling the ring almost cut into his skin. The Truthseeing was unlike anything he had ever experienced. Held fast in place, he grit his teeth as the Elf violated his mind, flicking through his memories, bringing them to light and then tossing them aside as if discarding books from a shelf.

'*Not the father, but perhaps the mother …*'

'*Get out of my head,*' said Wilhelm, swiping at the Elf's mind with his thoughts.

For a moment, the Elf recoiled. Then, rolling forward like a Western County storm, he smothered Wilhelm. Choking, gagging and then coughing, Wilhelm fought to breathe under the pressure, but the Elf was relentless, crushing Wilhelm beneath his power. After what seemed like an eternity, Wilhelm felt the sudden weightlessness of the Elf's retreat. He gulped at a great lungful of air and collapsed across the couch.

He could breathe again.

The slender Truthseer twirled his floor-length tunic of shining silver and moved to stand behind the desk. Spreading his decorated sleeves atop the desk, he leaned forward and stared at Wilhelm. Then, speaking with the confidence of someone used to being obeyed, he spoke to Wilhelm in the Ez language.

'I understand you made quite the commotion at Ezguard … It caused many people a great deal of pain. Much to the chagrin of the Councils, Grand Admiral Synnathril has requested you be taught to control your Truthseeing in an attempt to understand where it comes from.'

The Elf's hard grey eyes pierced Wilhelm as he fidgeted. Though no longer inside his mind, Wilhelm felt as though the aged Elf could still see everything.

'As I am sure you are well aware, the appearance of a Truthseeing Ez is an abomination. Your discovery has created quite the stir amongst the Councils, who are still debating your future. Despite what Grand Admiral Syn thinks, I believe you are unfit for training. You are too old, and you have far too restless a mind. We refuse to train Elves with an untamed mind like yours, as they make the most troubling students. But it would seem the Councils have backed the Grand Admiral's request, and so you will be trained.'

Wilhelm watched the Elf's creased face become thoughtful. 'Here is your first lesson. There is a mushroom that grows only in the caves beside the rapids of Torre. Find the mushroom, then return to me, and I will show you how to control your mind.'

'A mushroom will help me control my mind?' asked Wilhelm with a frown.

'That's not what I said,' said the Elf. 'Return to me with the mushroom, and I will show you how to control your power.'

'How will I know what I am looking for?'

'Blue cup and dark brown gills. It grows right on the water's edge. You will know it when you see it.'

Wilhelm's mind whirled. What would a mushroom do to his Truthseeing, and were the Elves really going to train him?

The Elf then turned from Wilhelm and waved his hand—a section of the bookshelf beside Wilhelm rolled aside, revealing a secret passage whose depths were hidden in darkness. Snapping his long Elven fingers, flames burst into existence within a number of lanterns along the passage wall. They illuminated a set of stone steps that descended from view.

Brushing his wispy hair back from his face, the Elf raised his thin eyebrows and waved his hands forward, as if to shoo Wilhelm down the stairs.

'Pyromancy …' said Wilhelm, frowning at the Elf. 'I thought an Elf could only control Truthseeing or mancery … not both.'

The Elf stopped to glare. 'I was using mancery to manipulate the world around me long before the Elves called it mancery, boy.' He pointed down the narrow passage. 'At the bottom of the steps you will find a small rowboat. Paddle from the grotto to the fast waters at the centre of the Torre River and travel downstream until you find the caverns. There, you will find the mushroom.'

Wilhelm allowed the tall Elf to push him toward the opening of the passageway, but stopping in the doorway, Wilhelm turned to face the Elf. 'I don't even know what to call you.'

'I am Neberadar, the Grand Librarian and Truthseer Supreme. Do not return without the mushroom.' The Elf waved a hand and the passage door slid back with a resounding boom.

Chapter Sixteen

WILHELM STARED DUMBFOUNDED at the closed stone door of the passage, trying to understand what had just happened. He peered over his shoulder at the flickering lanterns and frowned. He felt uneasy, a feeling distinct from his grief for Zethish. It was something else, something darker—as if sinister forces were at play.

He couldn't shake the feeling that the Elf wanted to be rid of him. And not just rid of him, but wanted him dead. Had it been anyone but an Elf, Wilhelm would have found their Truth in moments. But Neberadar's power eclipsed anything Wilhelm had ever experienced.

'*Begin your journey before I turn out the lights,*' the Elf's voice echoed through Wilhelm's mind.

The lantern beside his head extinguished with a small whoosh, and seconds later, the next followed. Accustomed to large, open spaces, Wilhelm couldn't bear the thought of being stuck in the unlit passage.

He sprinted towards the staircase and jumped down the treads two at a time as the lanterns extinguished behind at a quickening pace.

In full flight, he launched from the last stair and skidded onto the rocky shore of a subterranean grotto.

It was a small space, barely fifteen yards high, domed and mostly full of water. Wilhelm stopped to catch his breath and look at his surroundings. He stood atop a gravelly shore, with a rickety-looking jetty at its centre and a small rowboat berthed along-side the aged timbers. The boat bobbed gently on the water, and an oil lantern hung from the prow.

The shallow water reflected across the stone ceiling in beautiful patterns, and beyond the open-ing of the cave, Wilhelm could see the fast-flowing Torre River. The silvery moonlight showed how the water burbled and eddied in fast circular motions.

Wilhelm could tell he was outside the Elven city. He gazed at the silvery light dancing across the water, as he wondered why the mushroom was needed for him to leave Evenwood so suddenly. He wished Zethish were here. She would have known what to make of the Grand Librarian Neberadar and his strange request.

Thoughts of Zethish caused a tightness that spread across his chest. He could feel sorrow, pain and anger as they all vied for control of his thoughts. He pushed the emotions away, and in the hopes of distracting himself, Wilhelm climbed the timber steps, the aged wood creaking beneath his armoured boots.

There had been no opportunity to change out of his armour—he realised now—though it seemed unimportant. A wave of apathy washed over him. He shrugged; there was no point taking it off. Its weight felt comforting, and the fleece lining would keep him warm in the cool mountain air.

Stepping from the shifting timbers of the jetty, Wilhelm lowered himself to the bare innards of the tiny rowboat. His stomach growled like a panther, and he realised he couldn't remember the last time he'd eaten. Probably before they left for Ezguard; before Zethish's death.

A lump formed in his throat, but he steeled himself against more tears as he scanned the water. Resigned to his fate, he removed the slipknot from the jetty. There was no reason to stay here with nothing but his thoughts, and there was certainly nothing to eat in this barren grotto. Shuffling his backside to the correct seat, he resolved to find that Elf's stupid mushroom.

Wilhelm breathed evenly as he rowed from the grotto out into the bright moonlight and crisp mountain air. He felt a noticeable temperature drop and was thankful for the fleece lining of his armour. He drove the small boat toward the swift waters. He passed over a large eddy, and then the current grabbed the boat; with a firm jolt, the keel turned and accelerated downstream.

Wilhelm pulled in the oars and turned to face the direction of travel, watching as the strong current quickened the boat's pace. Closing his eyes, he inhaled the cold mountain air, hoping it would cleanse the pain he felt. Despite his best intentions, he let his mind wander back to Zethish, and as the memories of her took over, he lost track of time.

Down the Torre River, carving a path through the mountains of the Cradle, he lost contact with the real world. Time eluded him, as his mind wandered. He had no idea how long he travelled down the river, allowing the current to guide him. He existed only in his memories. He wanted her back; he would give anything to have her back.

Suddenly, the timber beneath his buttocks jolted, as the boat swerved on the water. Wiping his eyes, Wilhelm studied the river ahead and froze. It wasn't the sight that immediately alarmed him, but the sound of rushing water—rapids.

Realisation dawned. The Elf had said the caverns were beside the rapids. Wilhelm jerked into action as the small vessel bounced along the river. The Torre grew agitated, water frothing, throwing him from side to side as the river churned over submerged rocks. Grappling to hold himself upright in the rowboat, Wilhelm saw where sharp and jagged stone stuck out from the water. Glistening with the deadliest black, the rocks contrasted the white water foaming around them.

The current's grip already had him.

Wilhelm clutched at the sides of the boat, hoping to pin himself to the boat's centre. Left and right, sharp stones whizzed past, and all around him, water roared like a beast. The black rocks towered alongside him, wider than the boat's length as they passed by within a hand's width. A burst of acceleration, and the current carried him straight towards one of the largest rocks. Suddenly, he realised he'd misjudged just how huge they really were.

With his heart in his throat, Wilhelm braced for impact, but at the last moment, the hull swerved. On the twisting currents, he jolted around that massive rock and plunged into a maze of others.

Out of control, the boat weaved through rows of the glistening black stone. His hands gripped the sides with white knuckles, his heart pumping faster. Unsure whether he was thrilled or terrified, Wilhelm let out a nervous yelp as a wave of icy water coursed over the bow and hit his armoured torso with the force of a hammer blow. It drove the breath from his lungs and soaked him completely. He coughed and spluttered for air as the cold liquid poured off his face.

Another wave threw the small boat high into the air, and his stomach felt like it fell through the seat. And before he had a chance to react, a great splintering crack reverberated through him as the keel broke on a sharp rock.

His fingers scrabbled against the gunwales, latching on in the hope of stopping himself from being flung headfirst into the stone. He tried to hold the small boat together with sheer strength, but a second wave smashed into the hull. Shards of timber flew in every direction and sliced his unprotected face. His hands slipped, and he felt himself flying through the air before he slammed against another rock. Air gushed from his lungs in a pained grunt as he bounced off the wet surface and careened through the air again. With his arms and legs flailing, he skipped across the water before disappearing beneath the churning surface.

Clawing against the current, he felt his armour dragging him down. The heavy red-and-black protection had saved him from the worst of the impact, but now it pulled him towards his death.

He struggled to swim, fighting for the surface as the water around him shook him this way and that. Something jammed into his left side hard enough to dent his steel breastplate. Ribs crunched, but a spinning current swallowed his cries of pain as the water dragged him under even further. He tried to hold in his remaining air, but another howl escaped him as the swift water ground him along the gravel bottom.

He kicked off the riverbed to reach for freedom. He clamped his jaw shut, but it was coming. He could feel it as his arms thrashed at the water. The urge to breathe was just too strong.

And instinctively, his body took over.

He breathed. A great influx of freezing water gushed through his mouth into his lungs. The sudden realisation clasped at his insides with terror, its icy grip clutching at his life.

He was going to die.

With one last inhalation, his lungs filled, and his arms thrashed wildly around him. His vision narrowed, and as the blackness crept in, he felt the strength leave his body.

Warmth and a sudden relief flooded his last thought before death. *I'm coming, Zethish.*

CHAPTER SEVENTEEN

THE LONGER EZELL waited the more he cursed himself, his teachers and whoever else had organised this signal. His stomach grumbled in unison with his thoughts, and he promised himself that when he became King of the Ez, he would change the stupid procedure.

In a flurry of movement, the door to the tavern flung inwards, drawing Ezell's attention. A handsome male Ez of middle years strolled down the stairs. The Prince eyed the newcomer's broad shoulders and muscular torso as he turned in his direction. The man wore a matching set of tan breeches and tunic, an unmistakable dark swordbelt draped lazily around his athletic hips. Though the Ez strolled in a casual manner with his dark eyes fixed ahead, Ezell recognised a soldier when he saw one. Without making eye contact, the man walked past the Prince's table and continued to the bar, where he ordered a drink.

Ezell watched him go, eyeing his strong, muscular backside, and wondered if he was the contact. When the man downed his first drink, ordered a second and moved to a table on the other side of the seating area, Ezell decided not.

Tearing his eyes away from those muscles, Ezell jumped in fright so hard he hit the table loudly with his knees. There was a man sitting at the table with him.

'I didn't see you sit down,' stammered Ezell, trying to cover his discomfort with an awkward laugh. He rubbed his now aching knee. 'Where did you come from?'

The newcomer snatched at the tankard Ezell had left on the table as part of the signal to the Royal contact and tossed back the drink, gulping mouthful after mouthful. Ezell watched as some spilled around the cup's rim and onto the Ez's short, cropped beard before he slammed the cup down atop the table and burped loudly. 'You set up the signal.'

For a long moment, Ezell just stared at the newcomer in shock, wondering if this was truly the Royal contact, Dane Defolt. Finally, Ezell said the words: 'I did.'

'Why?' The dark-haired man asked.

'Do you know who I am?' said Ezell, trying hard to hide the anger that touched his voice.

The man's dark beady eyes focused on Ezell. 'Do you think a muddy face is enough to stop me from recognising the Crown Prince?'

Ezell shushed him loudly as he looked around the tavern, hoping to remain inconspicuous. 'Don't use my title.'

'Why not?' The Ez tilted his head at Ezell, and revealed a long scar that dragged its way from the right of his forehead, across his nose where it puckered in a mound of pink flesh and continued to his left cheek. His thin lips and tangled brows were turned down in what Ezell would have described as an eternal scowl.

'Because I told you not to,' said Ezell, staring into the Ez's bored expression. 'Are you the contact? Are you Defolt?'

The man sat in silence for a long time, his eyes boring into Ezell, before finally speaking. 'I am.'

'Good. I have a request of you.'

A noise like a hiccup escaped Defolt's mouth, and frowning, Ezell realised the scar across the man's face distracted him from seeing the smile that curled his lips. 'Is something amusing?' asked Ezell. He could feel anger rising in his chest.

'I don't work for you,' Defolt said, pulling the plate of food towards himself and picking up the utensils.

'What do you mean you don't work for me? You are the Royal Contact for Chancy and I,' Ezell lowered his voice to a whisper, 'am the Crown Prince. I have a request for you.'

'You're in exile … You're not a royal,' said Defolt.

Ezell's stomach grew cold.

The man smirked as he twirled the knife and fork like a parlour trick between them.

'News of your attack on the Human Governor and the new treaty spread like wildfire. The pigeons came the very same day. There's a King's ransom for your safe return,' he paused and smiled wolfishly at Ezell, 'or a Prince's ransom, anyway. I'd be rich if I turned you in.'

'I can't believe someone so disgustingly selfish works for my father,' said the Prince.

'Selfish? That's a bit rich coming from you, don't you think?'

'Excuse me?' Ezell fought to contain the rage that bubbled behind his words.

'Excuse you for what? Being an idiot? Do you want the Kingdom to break into a civil war? Because that's what it looks like to me. Go home, my Prince,' he said, leaning forward and tapping the table with the knife for emphasis. 'Go home and apologise to Daddy before I hand you in. Tell him you're sorry for being so silly and pretend this never happened.'

Ezell felt the colour rising to his face. 'You will regret the day you denied me this request, you ...' He struggled to think of the worst description he could muster. '...you brigand. I will never forget this insult, and when I am King—'

Dane threw his head back and laughed. 'You'll need to grow a set of balls first. Besides, you'll never make it that far, not at the rate you're—'

Ezell punched him square in the face. He stood as he delivered the blow, a powerful right hook that picked up the small-framed contact and threw him across the tavern. Then, tossing the table aside, he launched after the man and bellowed, 'How dare you!'

Before Ezell could land another punch, Defolt pulled himself from the floor and kicked out with his foot. The blow caught Ezell on one athletic thigh, and although it wasn't a disabling hit, it did throw him off balance. That was all Dane needed. In the moment it took Ezell to catch his balance, Defolt lunged forward, the knife clutched in his hands.

'You selfish brat!' Defolt feinted with the blade, testing Ezell's reaction speed. 'I bet you wanted me to contact the Elves to broker an alliance.'

Ezell danced left on the balls of his feet and pretended to throw a punch. 'You have no idea how important this is.'

'You're right, I don't, and the only thing keeping you alive right now is your father and the bounty on you. But that doesn't mean I can't hurt you.' Dane lunged, his blade arm outstretched.

Ezell pivoted—just like he had in the countless hours he'd spent in combat training—and grabbed the outstretched arm but felt only the fabric of the man's cuff as Defolt twisted away, far quicker than Ezell could move. Around him, he could hear the other patrons shouting, but their voices were distant, as he focused all of his attention on the swift knife fighter who danced back and forth before him.

Teasing with quick movements of the small blade, Defolt again lunged forward. Instead of trying to grab the man, Ezell sidestepped. Palming his blade arm so the attack flew wide, Ezell then used his advantage to scoop up a chair and throw it.

The wooden furniture crashed into Dane's back and splintered with a satisfying crunch that sent the small man sprawling across the floor. Ezell stood up to his full height when a thunk resonated within his skull. Instantly, his vision blurred as he staggered forward a step and fell to his knees. An armoured hand then grabbed his head, and a baton slid around his neck that squeezed against his windpipe.

A soldier dressed in shining armour stepped into Ezell's swirling vision, a white castle emblazoned on his breastplate. He pointed a loaded crossbow at the Prince's chest and said, 'Cease and desist at once.'

The sounds of scuffling drifted into Ezell's ringing ears. 'Get your dirty mitts off. He's mine. The bounty is mine!'

'Shut up,' said a third Guard, backhanding Dane across his already bruising face, the armoured glove ringing on impact. 'Under the rule of Count Tobias Borlonn, brawling is illegal. As citizens and visitors of the Northern County, it is your duty to read and understand our laws. You are both under arrest.'

'Do not resist. You will only make this harder,' said the Guard from behind Ezell, and even with his head still ringing, Ezell could hear the excitement in the Guard's voice.

A black bag that smelled like sweat was then pulled over his head, obliterating any distinct sight or sound.

The Guards of Chancy then pulled him to his feet, placed manacles around his wrists and walked him up the stairs. Unceremoniously, they tossed him next to Defolt into the back of what he could only assume was a carriage.

The hard timber beneath his backside jolted, and through the material, Ezell could hear the undeniable clocking of hooves on cobblestones. Beside him, Dane squirmed and cursed Ezell's name as he jabbed an elbow into the Prince's side.

'Shut up,' growled the Prince. 'You're not helping.'

'You shut up.' Dane's voice came muffled. 'Once they see who I am, I'll be set free. But once they see you ...'

'You'd better hope that is the case,' said Ezell, 'because if I ever see your ugly, scarred face again, it will be the last thing you remember. Ever.'

Ezell tried to feel as certain as he sounded, but cold dread seeped through his stomach. As the carriage continued to bounce along the cobblestones, he attempted to reposition his weight several times, but at each instance, he failed in the tight restraints. Growing frustrated, he lashed out at Defolt. 'Get your elbow out of my ribs, or I'll remove it for you.'

Dane retorted and started bickering, kicking and pushing at Ezell in the tight confines of the carriage until it squeaked to a halt and they were hauled and tossed onto the cobblestones.

Ezell had no idea where he was. He'd lost his sense of direction long before in the twisting streets of the White City. The guardsman manhandled him up a set of stone steps and across a threshold into what sounded like an enormous hall. Sounds of their passage bounced and reflected all around them, so Ezell thought they must be in a large ornate building. His stomach dropped even further, it had to be one of the castles.

The Guards of Chancy continued to lead them in silence until they stopped abruptly, their breathing even and marked. A voice, regal and commanding filled the space, 'Unhand him at once. Exile or not, he is still the Crown Prince of the Ez. The other is known to me. Let him go.'

Suddenly, in a blast of bright light, the bag was removed.

'He is mine, sire,' said Defolt. 'I found him, so the bounty is mine!'

'You will have your bounty, now get out of my sight.'

Dazzled, Ezell blinked and rubbed at his wrists as the manacles fell away. He turned to watch as Defolt, looking disgruntled at his treatment, walked towards a set of massive wooden doors. The man winked teasingly at Ezell and gave him a rude gesture before sliding a finger across his throat. Biting down his frustration, Ezell watched the doors close, then turned to his surroundings.

Before him stood a broad-shouldered, sturdy figure draped in white and gold finery. His aged form was accentuated by his clothing, with a sash pulled tight about his middle, lines of golden thread that stretched from his waist up to edge his shoulders and a white cape that fell from the silver clasp at his neck.

He stared into the hard green eyes before him and instantly recognised the man's neatly trimmed goatee and tightly pursed lips. 'Count Borlonn. Had I known I would be in the presence of an Ez Lord, I would have dressed for the occasion.' He held the Count's gaze, determinded, 'or bathed at least.'

Count Borlonn regarded Ezell with an upturned nose, and with a swoosh of his cape, he turned his back.

Ezell eyed the white cape and decided he would have laughed if the mood wasn't so serious. The outfit would have looked at home in the fairy tale representation of a prince from the Sand Tribes of Ver Dunn, far to the west of the Border Ranges.

'Your poor attempt at humour will do little to ease the tension, Prince Ezell,' said Count Borlonn.

Despite the apprehension rising in his stomach, Ezell couldn't help but feel impressed at the surrounding audience chamber. It was massive, with its glass wall overlooking the city and the ornamental ceiling far above. Threading across the space above him were balconies and spiral staircases of the finest carved timber, decorated with the busts of beasts from the Western County. Despite the oppressive amount of dark red timber covering the floor, walls and ceiling of the vast space, Ezell felt the large fireplaces lent a soft, homey feel.

Though there was a lavish display of tapestries, and more examples of the clothing that the Count wore were showcased upon sets of stuffed dummies, Ezell's gaze was drawn back to where the Count stood before his ornate throne. It wasn't the throne that caught his eye, but the single, four-storey high glass window Ezell had seen from the other side of the ravine.

From where he stood in the spacious audience chamber, he could see most—if not all—of the White City, flowing down the valley wall, and back up the other side, the Castle Valerius sitting proudly opposite. He held his breath; Chancy was truly a sight to behold.

The sound of Count Borlonn's voice drew Ezell's attention. 'How do you find the White City, Ezell, Prince in Exile?'

Ezell squared his jaw and as the Count turned around, he met the man's hard, green eyes. 'Despite our differences, Count Borlonn, I can honestly say this is one of the most beautiful Ez cities I've seen.'

'It *is* the most beautiful,' Borlonn corrected him. 'I do, however, wish the circumstances of your visit weren't so undesirable.'

'What are you going to do with me?' said Ezell, as he again rubbed where the manacles had chafed his wrists.

'Oh please,' Borlonn looked genuinely hurt, 'we're not barbarians. You will simply remain my guest until your father can be notified. He will decide what to do with you.'

As if on cue, the wooden doors behind Ezell creaked open, and a soldier entered. Without a helm, he wore full body armour coloured in the same pure—pompous—white as the Count. Ezell eyed the soldier's masculine form beneath his armour and his sharp, attractive features. Across his breastplate, golden vines laid in a delicate tracework glittered with his every step. The blond-haired soldier regarded Ezell with bright green eyes as he passed, marching straight to Borlonn's side. Ezell stared at the Ez's hair colour and realised it had been a long time since he'd met another blond-haired Ez.

'My Lord,' the soldier said with a bow, 'you requested my presence?'

'Indeed, but first, your manners. I would like to introduce you to Prince Ezell, now the Prince in Exile. And my Prince Ezell,' Borlonn continued, 'please be acquainted with one of my most trusted advisers, Alexander of Chancy.'

The soldier bowed deeply, his green eyes watching Ezell with interest as he bent in half. 'My Prince.'

Ezell nodded his head, refusing to bow. 'Alexander of Chancy, I don't believe I have heard your name before. From where do you hail?'

The soldier's back straightened beneath his gold-encrusted armour, and Borlonn stepped in to answer. 'Alexander is my ward. After an unfortunate upbringing, I brought him to the castle and sponsored him under my name. He has since proved himself as willing and as capable as any son. He is well cared for under my roof with his three adopted sisters.'

Borlonn shared a knowing look with his adopted son. 'Unfortunately, my own daughters also suffered a great loss during their upbringing, with the death of their mother. I believe the four of my family find solace and understanding in one another. Wouldn't you agree, Alexander?'

The soldier broke his green eyes away from Ezell—for only the barest moment—as he nodded to the Count.

'Please trust me when I say, my Prince,' continued Borlonn, 'I would have introduced my three daughters to you as well, had my eldest not recently caused a scene and disappeared from the castle.'

Ezell raised his eyebrows in question.

The Count sighed deeply. 'I fear she takes after her mother and shares her unstable nature. My wife took her own life shortly after the birth of our third girl, M'Lea.'

Ezell recalled that sad tale, drifting through the courts of Ezguard more than fifteen years ago when he was just a boy.

The Count waved dismissively. 'It was a long time ago now, but I still mourn her. I wonder if the looming war has put pressure on my eldest, Lyren, and pushed her towards an action we will all regret.'

'Do you have any idea where she has gone?' asked Ezell, genuine concern rising in his chest.

Alexander answered with serious features but a soft voice. His eyes lingered on Ezell, 'She was last seen heading east on horseback, and although we've sent many soldiers to search, we are yet to find her.'

'I believe she's gone into the Ghost Country,' added the Count. 'Many refuse to enter those haunted woods.'

'You don't honestly believe the tales?' Ezell scoffed. 'They're told to scare children so they don't run off.'

Borlonn's back stiffened, and his eyes slitted at the Prince. 'I am old enough to remember the Necromancer's War, boy. I have spent every year of my life here in the Northern County, and I can promise you, I know its every hill and stream better than you ever will. Those tales were born of truth, so mark my words when I say there is a mystic power in the Ghost Country.'

Ezell, hoping he seemed sincere, simply nodded and waited as the Count and Alexander measured him with their eyes. Ezell took the moments to follow the lines of Alexander's features. He was a handsome Ez, with thin eyebrows and serious green eyes. A strong, pointed nose, a set of pursued lips, and his squared jaw was shaved to the skin. Long seconds passed before Borlonn turned to Alexander. 'Have a message sent to the capital by pigeon at once. Inform the King we have captured his son.'

'Ah, I would, my Lord, but there's a problem in the aviary tower.'

'What problem?' said Borlonn.

'The pigeons are gone, my Lord, all of them,' said Alexander. 'The Guards are investigating it as we speak, but we believe foul play.'

'To the Old Hells with them,' the Count cursed. 'Send a messenger carriage and a small contingent of mounted troops immediately. If the pigeons return, send them as well. The King needs to know as soon as possible.'

'By your command, my Lord,' the young Ez bowed and strode past Ezell, his green eyes running up and down the Prince with interest.

Ezell watched the atrractive young Ez leave, his every lithe move catching the Prince's eye.

Count Borlonn turned and held his back to Ezell until the creaking doors signalled Alexander's departure. He then rounded on the Prince with flashing eyes. 'See what you have started?'

'What?' said Ezell, still thinking about the handsome Alexander of Chancy. 'I wasn't anywhere near your aviary.'

'The entire realm heard how you defied the King's orders and took a stand against him. Think about how that may have been received by the Ez people.'

Ezell frowned and shook his head. 'What are you talking about?'

'There are some who saw your act of defiance as an opportunity to do as they please, forgoing the law to take matters into their own hands.'

'You mean like vigilantes?'

'I mean villains,' said the Count heatedly. 'You've given power to the lowest levels of society, showing them it's okay to subjugate the King's decisions. You've given the power to those who shouldn't have it.'

Ezell squared his jaw. 'They're all Ez citizens, Count Borlonn. They aren't villains.'

'Well, they *weren't* villains, but you gave them a reason to be.'

Ezell couldn't help but smile. 'This is ridiculous. I didn't give them a reason to do anything, I gave them hope.'

'Hope for what?' The Count turned on his heel and began pacing back and forth. 'Chaos and a future without order is all I see.'

'Hope for a future free of oppression.'

'That is exactly what your father is working on. Joining the Human Alliance—'

Ezell interjected. 'We have no idea what the Humans want or what the terms of the treaty are.'

He paused and read the Count's quickly schooled expression. 'You know, don't you?'

'I do.'

'And?' Ezell crossed his arms and straightened his back.

'It is not my place to reveal such things to you. You are the Prince in Exile.'

'Who else knows of the treaty?'

'All four County Lords and the King agreed unanimously. We accepted the terms and saw it as the most responsible option for removing ourselves from the Elven reign without the threat of war.'

'Without the threat of war?' Ezell repeated, his voice rising in volume. 'Only because the Humans will fight the war for us.'

'Is there something wrong with that? I see no problem committing their soldiers to a war we do not want.'

'We need to earn our freedom, and that includes freedom from the Elves and the Humans,' Ezell said, glaring at the Count.

'There is never a *need* for war. This treaty—'

'What did you offer them in return for their support?' Ezell interrupted again. 'Tell me. I am an exile and soon to be returned to my father. What harm could it do? What did the County Lords and my father give to the Humans as part of the treaty?'

Borlonn's hard green eyes glared at Ezell for several moments. 'We gave them farming land. Well, more precisely, we sold them farming land. They needed the fields to support their people, so everything south of Granville now belongs to the Humans.'

Ezell's mouth fell open and his mind froze. He stammered over his next words, struggling to make his mouth move. 'You gave them *all* of it?'

'No, weren't you listening, I said we sold it to them. And in return, they showed us what they have in store for the Elves.' Borlonn chortled low in his chest. 'I am personally opposed to the notion of war, but even I have to admit, it is a fitting and ironic end to the Elven rule.'

Ezell's head swam. 'All of that land.' He struggled to calculate the extent they were talking about. 'What about the people? That's thousands of people, thousands of Ez families whose homes you just took away. You stole it from them to support a race we know nothing about.'

'Don't be so dramatic.' Borlonn's lip curled in disgust. 'It is a notion of trust. Besides, we Lords compensated each and every family financially. They will be given new land and relocated here to the Northern or Eastern County. There is more than enough land to—'

'That soil is dry and unfit for farming.' Ezell spoke over the Count. 'It's nothing like the soil around Granville. The Southern County is our best farming land.' Ezell turned away and put his hands to his head, struggling to understand. 'Why would my father give away our highest-producing land? This is madness.'

'You are overly emotional for a Prince and not at all like your father. This is not madness, it's called negotiation. A way of coexisting without resulting in war with the Humans. For if we are not with them, we will be arrayed against them, and we have no army to fight them.'

'You are such a pacifist,' Ezell said the word like it was the worst thing he could have said.

Borlonn recoiled as if physically hit and then shook his head, greying hair swaying in the light. 'I remember your father being so proud of you when you were young. He saw so much potential, and now look at you. You're barely a man, and already you are a disgrace.' Borlonn gestured at the Prince as if too disgusted to look at him, face twisted into a scowl. 'You are nothing but a criminal seeking to spread dissent and unease across our nation. A child too ignorant to face reality like a man.'

The Prince crossed his arms and narrowed his eyes. 'I could say the same of you, Count Borlonn. The only difference I see between myself and the County Lords is that you have all retained your titles and comforts. At least I have enough strength in my belief to fight for our people, no matter the personal cost.'

'This decision is a compromise reached through extensive negotiation. It took us a great deal of time to finalise our decision, and I agree it is not ideal, but that is the nature of compromise. It is about working together towards a common goal, something you seem adamant to destroy. This treaty is a far better option than starting a war with the Elves or the Humans. It is a peaceful and responsible solution. We are paving the way for our future, a future where all Ez are free to choose their own destinies.'

'But not their own homes … You'll choose that for them.'

Count Borlonn opened his mouth and then closed it again, clearly agitated. 'I thought I could talk to you, Prince Ezell. I thought I could reason with you and discuss the errors of your actions. But clearly, I am mistaken, because you are without conscience and foresight. You are a child.'

Ezell took a step forward, his finger held before him, and his lips pursed tightly. 'You say that, sitting upon your throne and draped in your finery as you take homes away from the people. And you say I am without conscience?'

'It is my land to take!' bellowed the Count, swiping his hands across his body as spit flew from his mouth. 'We are the Lords of the Ez, and it is our responsibility to create a future for all our charges. Don't you dare stand there pretending you are without fault, Prince Ezell. You are meant to be a protector of the Ez, but instead, you're spreading dissent among the nation like the Blue Plague. You *must* see where your little insurrection will lead, for there is only one outcome. You will divide the nation and push us into civil war on top of the Human and Elf war. You will tear Belissia apart.'

'You can't pacify your way around every problem, Count, including me. We need this conflict, whether you see it or not. The Ez need to wake up and realise it's time to fight for their freedom. We can't sit back and watch someone else fight our battles, because freedom must be earned. The future is upon us and—' Ezell stopped mid-thought.

On the verge of revealing Wilhelm's secret, Ezell realised his mistake. He wanted to explain to the old fool that there were Ez who'd discovered the power of Truthseeing. He wanted to tell Borlonn that young Wilhelm went to train with the Elves and that Ezell had every intention of working with them. That once Wilhelm knew more about his power, he would be the key to the Ez winning their freedom. But he couldn't. Not yet. The time wasn't right.

'Fight for our own survival,' said the Count with a laugh that echoed around the room. 'You have no idea what you're speaking of. There's no way we'd win fighting for our survival.'

'So ironic,' Ezell said as he crossed his arms.

'What is?' Venom dripped from Borlonn's words.

'You and your pacifist ways are pushing us towards a war not of our choosing. Whether you like it or not, Borlonn, war is coming. We *will* be dragged in, and we will all have to choose a side.'

'No, Prince Ezell. You are the one pushing us toward this apparent war, and it is you that is driving a wedge between the Ez people. And when thousands of innocents do die in your war, you alone will be responsible.' The Count waved to signal the guards who stood waiting at the doors.

'If news of my actions have spread as far as you say, then my father's reign is weaker than he thinks. The Ez are already as divided as you and I, Count Borlon, and you know it. I am not the one spreading dissent, I am simply giving voice to those without one.'

With clanking armour, the Guards of Chancy grabbed Ezell by the arms, their gauntlet hands clamping down hard on his skin. But Ezell kept talking. 'Including those you uprooted in the Southern County, Borlonn. Wait until the rest of the Ez hear about that!'

The Count exhaled and shook his head. 'Lock him away until his Father comes for him.'

Chapter Eighteen

GRAND ADMIRAL SYNNATHRIL bowed respectfully to Princess Dianella and bid his farewell. Turning on his heel, he rubbed at his tired eyes and strode away from the Council Chambers. He began the long walk to his quarters, far above on the surface of Evenwood. As usual, the Council sessions after Selouteau's hearing had been long and frustrating, dragging on until no single Council member possessed the energy to continue.

The Traditionalists and the Integrists had once again struggled to come to any compromise, and so the Elves remained undecided on how to deal with the Human threat. Syn felt himself hoping the Humans would attack, if only to draw a cohesive reaction from the Councils.

He longed for strong leadership—a figurehead the Elves could rally behind, one they could follow into battle. But he knew those days were long gone. The Councils would never condone a course of action that would place themselves directly in harm's way. They were too content to sit on their thrones debating.

Syn wished King Eltavar would disband the Councils in favour of a singular elective monarchy. He felt such a decision would remove all their political problems, both within their doors and outside in the greater Belissia.

He liked to think *he*, as an elected monarch, would have organised a swift campaign into Ezguard the moment he learned the Governor's location. He would have removed the head of the beast cleanly. Yet, bound to the throne as a Council member, he could not. Not without reverting to treasonous acts with Selouteau.

Currently, outside of the Elven Councils, King Elvatar was the prevailing decision maker for all Belissia. However, the problem resided in how King Eltavar remained removed from the debate, as the Councils bickered amongst themselves like children.

Since their arrival on Belissian soil, Syn had participated in the debate on how to deal with the Humans. He had hoped he could influence their decisions well enough to coax a stronger reaction— the correct reaction—but he'd made no ground.

Every day, he suggested and offered opinions that were swatted aside in the fierce debate between parties, while in the real world, Syn believed the Humans were preparing to invade. It was maddening. He sat at the pinnacle of the Elven race with his hands tied, unable to do what he thought was right. And so, time and time again, he'd taken matters into his own hands, by whatever means necessary.

Permitting Selouteau to enter Ezguard in an attempt to capture the Governor had been one event in a long line of indiscretions, but they were for the benefit of all.

Turning a corner he exhaled sharply, hoping to rid himself of the irritation within.

Up ahead, whispered voices drifted down the corridor and caught Syn's attention. If there was one thing he'd learned from his time in the Councils, it was that whispers meant secrets, and secrets meant power.

Slowing his pace, Syn tiptoed to the corner. He pressed his back against the cool stone of the subterranean passage and stretched his long ears to the murmured words ahead.

'Of course, I dealt with him, Eltavar. Don't you dare admonish me like a child. I've been in this game just as long as you.'

'Then you also know how important this is. Has it been done?'

Even from around the corner, Syn could feel the melodramatic delivery of the words that followed. *Neberadar,* Syn thought, being careful to calm his mind against the Grand Librarian's Truthseeing.

'I directed that Ez toward the Torre to forage for mushrooms. I explained it would be required for the training.'

'You sent him to search for mushrooms?'

'I improvised,' said Neberadar in a dramatic way. 'Suffice to say, he took the boat into the Torre, and I found its remains scattered about the rapids. I took the liberty to ensure he still wore his armour with a slight push of Truthseeing. He has surely drowned.'

'And you're sure?'

'Again, the admonishment, chastising me like some child. He wore his armour, Eltavar. I scoured the scene myself and couldn't feel his mind. He is dead.'

'You're sure?'

'I have a mind to slap you. A quick blow to the head to remove this disgusting attitude you have developed. He is dead. Is there any other way I can describe it so you will hear what I am saying?'

'I simply want to be sure this time, Neberadar. The re-emergence of the Truthseeing Ez is something we cannot afford to deal with right now. We have more pressing matters at hand.'

'Yes, of course, the Humans. Do you think it is Ollanar coming to test us?' Neberadar said.

'I would surely bet on it.'

'But why now? Why after so long?'

'You know the answer as well as I, Neberadar; the clock is ticking. We have less than forty years until the return of the Purge. He is sending us a message, testing our resolve to decide who will protect us from its return. This is a message we can only reply to in kind,' Eltavar said, a deliberate edge to his voice.

'And the other artefacts … Do you truly believe they are here, on Belissian soil?'

'Bissah was cunning and trapped, so we have no idea where she hid them. But if we are to escape the Purge and get off this Oblivion spawned rock, we will need to find them again.'

Syn heard the shuffling of feet as they turned and walked further down the passage, away from where he hid.

'Speaking of artefacts, have you seen my ring?' Neberadar's voice sounded distant.

'The Orb?' questioned Eltavar.

'Yes, the Orb,' Neberadar snapped. 'I seem to have misplaced it.'

'You're getting old, and your mind is wandering. It can't have gone far.'

The Grand Librarian's reply was lost on Syn's ears as the speakers disappeared down the next passage.

Syn clenched his fists as fury burned through his veins. He stepped from around the corner into the centre of the hallway, the flickering of Pyromancy dancing to life within his curled fingers. They'd lied. They knew the Human leader and why he'd come for war, and they knew about the artefacts. They'd murdered Wilhelm and said that this was the re-emergence of the Truthseeing Ez—which meant it had happened before!

He crushed the bright flame within his fingers. Syn wanted to scream, but he knew he must calm himself, lest Neberadar feel his strong emotions with Truthseeing. His beautiful wife Selenna had always been the emotional one of the two. Quick to anger and quick to act, it was what had attracted Syn to the beautiful Elf.

He let the image of her golden-brown eyes ease his heart rate, and as his mind slowed, he took a breath. Years of working with the Councils had taught him to live to fight for another day and to strike when they were weakest. He needed time to think.

His thoughts turned to his daughter Selouteau and how she had lied to the Council of the Admirals of the Elven Armada; she was treading a new path, and she still needed him. He wouldn't do anything rash; not yet. He began walking, weaving his way deeper into Evenwood's underground, a plan brewing in his thoughts.

Finding a distant room where swirls of dust indicated that no Elf had used the chamber for a long time, Grand Admiral Synnathril shut the stone door behind him. He cast his eyes about the small room—an empty teaching area with workspaces and seating scattered about. Kicking the closest desk aside with a well-placed boot, he cleared a space, and then delved deep into his memory for the symbols he would need.

Certain he remembered everything correctly, the Grand Admiral took his thin dagger from its scabbard, and with a precise flick, he sliced open his left wrist.

Gritting his teeth and pumping his fist, Syn worked the blood downwards so it dripped steadily to the floor, where he spread the warm red liquid into a circle. He then drew four symbols at the centre and checked the strokes before tying a handkerchief over his wound.

It had been a long time since he'd sworn to never use Necromancy again, and the last time he'd seen his friend, Vylok. After the Necromancer's atrocities and the tens of thousands of deaths he'd instigated with his armies of Shadowbeasts, Syn couldn't continue practising Necromancy with good conscience. But this was different.

He closed his eyes in concentration and extended his senses to where he felt an answering power. Necromancy was the darkest of all Elven mancery. Painful and bloody, but when employed correctly, it was uniquely powerful and dangerous. A skilled Necromancer could open the way between this world and the Shadow Realm using the power in their blood, and through the portals, Shadowbeasts and Shades could be conjured.

Of course, the Beasts would always fight to resist their captor and turn on them in an attempt to break free. And more than once in their youth, Syn and Vylok had needed to hunt down and kill a renegade Beast they'd failed to control. But over time, they'd learnt to command them with the runes he'd now inscribed on the floor.

Syn shook his head, clearing his mind of any thoughts of his old friend. If he was to have any chance of finding Wilhelm before his soul passed through the Shadow Realm, Syn needed to enter in person. And for that, he needed his wits about him.

The energy of the Shadow Realm flowed through his Necromancy in rippling waves, which meant the portal was stable. Syn brandished his sword and summoned forth a ball of his Pyromancy that hung on the air above his hand. Taking a deep breath, he pushed forward through the wall of energy that rippled above the blood circle. It was the portal to the Shadow Realm. Stepping into it was like a wall of spiderwebs, but taking another step, the sensation was gone.

Syn was in the Shadow Realm.

The first thing he saw was red—a swirling mass of crimson smoke that billowed and eddied around him. Next, he smelled the stench of old blood, as shapes materialised through the haze. They darted this way and that, but remained always out of focus and reach; just.

He took a few steps away from the portal, conscious of the despair that permeated this world. He'd forgotten how the dense emotions came—smothering—despair and hatred, so powerful that they pressed on his mind.

He called out for Wilhelm, and his voice came as a hollow noise; muffled and seemingly carrying only a few feet.

All around him, the phantoms grew agitated as they became aware of his presence, flitting close but never close enough to see or touch.

Syn watched them with wary eyes as he stepped a little further into the red mist. He felt its dampness on his face and saw where the red liquid formed on his skin. His heart rate quickened, and with a shortened breath, he called a second time, but Wilhelm's soul did not respond.

Syn looked around. He knew he couldn't last much longer in this place, lest he become lost in the despair. He'd read enough about those who lingered for too long in the Shadow Realm …

He knew that the Old Gods of the Ez considered the Shadow Realm an afterlife of sorts. They thought it a place of safekeeping for those needing to exhaust the emotional turmoil caused by death's torture. And that, in this world, broken souls would pause on their way to a true afterlife—to cleanse their woes.

From his time spent observing the happenings of the Shadow Realm, he knew the Truth in those stories. He saw souls, fresh from death, writhing in the trauma of their passing. They screamed as they came to terms with their own death, forced to make a choice—accept their fate and move on to the afterlife, or become devoured by it.

Too many times, Syn had watched them morph into something dark and terrifying, consumed by the hatred of their demise. They mutated into creatures bent on unleashing their inconsolable rage on everything around them.

In the pages of the Necromantic Tome, Syn and Vylok had learned that what was left of those souls became Shades. Studying them, they found their nature powerful, devious and infinitely more cunning than that of the Shadowbeasts. But with the right amount of persuasion, power and concentration, these Shades could be shackled to become loyal soldiers, able to move across the Shadow Realm and do their bidding. Even search for a dead, Truthseeing Ez.

If Syn could bind a Shade to his will, he could employ its power to track Wilhelm's soul. Then, with Necromancy, the Ez could return to the world of the living, where he could learn to control his powers and help move Belissia toward a future the Lesser Races deserved.

He turned back to the portal, from where it would be safer to call forth a Shade. But as he moved, a shadow—lithe and fast—brushed by his consciousness and raced for the portal. It was a Shade—fleetingly quick—and its touch triggered his memories of a happier time with his wife, filled with love. For the briefest of moments, he became lost in those thoughts; he longed to stay and enjoy them, but the Shade was heading straight for his portal.

He had to stop it. There was no telling what would happen if a Shade was released on the world.

Sprinting forward, Syn launched himself through the portal. But it was too late. The Shade was already there. It was tethered by the power of the blood circle, but it could still attack.

Tendrils of orange mancery leapt from the Shade and began smashing about the room. Every surface they touched caught alight with flames of brilliant orange. Syn brought his sword up to attack, but a blast of orange mancery cracked across his chest, throwing him backwards against a wall. He fell across the piled desks and chairs that were burning from the Shade's mancery, as the creature continued the attack.

Rolling aside, Syn hurled a flaming ball of Pyromancy and watched as the Shade deflected his power aside with ease. Suddenly, Syn's breath caught in his throat as he recognised the Shade.

'Selenna!' Syn threw down his sword and held his hands up in surrender. 'Selenna, it's me!' called Syn, as the deadly energy swept toward him. At the last second, it shattered into a thousand tiny lights that fell from the air like rain. There, amid the falling pinpricks of energy, he forced his eyes to focus. 'Selenna, don't you recognise me?'

'You're a Necromancer,' said the voice of his long-dead wife, her eyes glowing from beneath the dark hood of her cloak.

He laughed nervously. 'Selenna, it's been fifty years since I last saw you, and that's the first thing you say to me?'

'What do you want me to say, Syn?'

'As your husband, I would have thought I'd deserve something a little more ... loving.' He took a step forward with his hands outstretched.

'Our vows were clear, Syn. Till death and not beyond.'

'Are you ...' he stopped, unsure if he could say the words aloud. 'Are you a Shade?'

His eyes adjusted from the explosions of mancery, and he studied her beautiful face. She hadn't aged a day.

Her eyes dipped.

'After fifty years in the Shadow Realm, I don't know what I am anymore ...' Her voice trailed off. She glanced up from the floor to stare at him, then pushed back the hood from her head. His eyes travelled down the long black length of her hair as it spilled around her face. She was just as beautiful as he remembered.

'The Councils said you and all the Inquisitors died detaining Vylok. How did you survive?'

She laughed without humour. 'I would hardly call this surviving.'

'We can figure something—'

'Don't you dare use your Necromancy on me!' she shrieked.

Syn flinched, and even without any Truthseeing power, he could feel the hot wash of her anger. He watched her pause, and when she spoke again, her voice was thick with emotion. It reminded him just how powerful she was.

'I fought the evil of Necromancy with everything that I had … and now, my own husband is using it, calling forth Shades from the Shadow Realm.'

'Selenna, my love,' he said, holding his hands in plea, 'so much has changed. Please let me explain why I'm here, and know with all my love that I have come to the end of my tether. This,' he opened his arms to the circle of blood, 'was my last option.'

She gazed steadily at Syn, the barest softening of her eyes the only indication she had allowed him to continue.

He nodded and smiled warmly, as emotions he hadn't experienced for five decades stirred within him. 'It's good to see you again, Selenna.'

'Get on with it.'

He began slowly, not sure where to start. He opened with her apparent death and how the Councils alleged that she and all the Inquisitors were killed while detaining the Necromancer.

'That is not how it happened,' she said, but when he looked at her questioningly, she fell silent. He went on, briefly touching on the fifty years of peace since Vylok's demise.

'That was your doing, Selenna. You brought peace to Belissia.' He grew uneasy as her expression hardened and quickly continued with news of their daughter, Selouteau, and how she had risen to the rank of Captain with a ship of her own.

'She was always so clever,' said Selenna.

'Just like her mother,' he ventured.

'Don't push your luck.' She fixed him with a cold stare.

He pressed on, updating her on the Humans' arrival, the trade treaties of the Southern Islander cities, the Prince of the Ez's exile and the Ez King joining the Human Alliance, all of which had finally escalated into the beginnings of another war.

'The Humans?' she hissed.

'You know about them?'

'We encountered them while tracking Vylok. I judged their technology threatening and sent word to the Councils. But they never replied.' She paused to rake him with her golden-brown eyes, 'Why Necromancy, Syn?'

'I'm getting there.' He smiled briefly, nerves fluttering in his stomach. 'During the failed mission to Ezguard, Selouteau encountered a Truthseeing Ez.' He waited to judge her reaction before moving on, but she gave nothing away. So he continued. 'I ordered him back to Evenwood so we could learn where his power comes from … I could see the emergence of other Truthseeing Ez as the push the Lesser Races need to break free of the Councils. But King Eltavar and the Grand Librarian Neberadar murdered him. They murdered him, Selenna.'

'Yes, I heard you. So you thought to catch him in the Shadow Realm?' She pointed at the bloody arc surrounding her, binding her within his power.

'I hoped he would reveal there were more like him. It's the next chapter of Belissian history, Selenna. Other races with the power of mancery. Just think of the possibilities.'

'Just think of the war, Syn. Centuries of hate spilling across the land. You know the Councils would never allow it. The King has already made his intentions clear. But you were prepared to have them trained without the Councils knowing, weren't you?'

'It wouldn't be the first time I've operated without their permission,' said Syn.

'And what then, Synnathril? What do you plan to do with your Truthseeing Ez? Incite a revolution and create a civil war, so *you* can sit on the throne?'

Anger flashed within him, and he struggled to find an answer. He'd thought something similar only moments before. 'Resolutions rarely appear without conflict, Selenna. You of all people know that. And conflict resolution is far the better option than unresolved conflict bubbling under the surface until it explodes.'

She stared at him, the workings of her mind evident behind her eyes. 'I'm sorry. I know you wouldn't set out to start a war. I know you well enough to understand you're *trying* to do the right thing.'

Syn felt relief that his wife hadn't completely succumbed to being a Shade. 'Can you find him in the Shadow Realm?'

'He's not in the Shadow Realm,' she said.

'But Neberadar said he was dead. Surely, he hasn't recovered from the emotional trauma of death already? Surely, he hasn't moved on?'

'I know every red rock in there like the back of my hand, Syn. I've been stuck there for an eternity, and I'm telling you,' her voice escalated, 'that this Truthseeing Ez is not in the Shadow Realm!'

He held a placating hand towards her as his mind raced with the possibilities, 'Perhaps the old Elf was mistaken and the Ez remains alive. Could you find him in this world?'

She pointed to the blood circle still surrounding her feet. 'Not shackled to your will, I won't. I am not some Shade from the Shadow Realm to be leashed to your heel, Syn.'

His mind grew troubled. Was she playing some kind of trick? Shades were nasty, malevolent beings, but this was his wife …

'Syn,' her voice took on a dangerous edge, 'you know you aren't powerful enough to stop me. Even if I am a Shade, you could never truly shackle me to your will.' She paused to let her words take hold. 'Free me, and I will find your Truthseeing Ez. I will protect him when you cannot.'

He frowned at her but strode forward, crouched to the circle of blood and wiped at a section of the arc. Instantly, his mind eased as the Necromancy faded behind Selenna, the waves rippling from the

Shadow Realm disappeared, and she was freed of his will.

She inhaled deeply, and her outline become more defined and less of a smoky, intangible haze. She reached back and pulled the dark hood up over her head so only her eyes were visible within.

He peered into her golden-brown eyes, his thoughts racing. 'I have so many questions.'

'In time, Syn,' she said, brushing the side of his face. 'But it is good to see you again.'

Then, in an explosion of black particles that drifted down to settle around him, she disappeared.

CHAPTER NINETEEN

CIƆ

WREADALLANON'S EYES SNAPPED open, and he looked at the cell around him. The Councils still had him in custody, trying to decide his fate for attacking the Human Governor.

Groaning through the pain, he shuffled his clammy, aching body across the cell's floor; his lower back cramped. He scraped the sparse hay into something resembling a pillow. It had been another nightmare he couldn't remember that had woken him, and as his consciousness resurfaced, the wisps of the nightmare drifted away.

Hard, unkind stone, barely softened by the thin layer of straw, resisted his search for a comfortable position. He grimaced; they hadn't designed the cells of Evenwood with the comfort of their charges in mind.

'I suppose I had better get used to it,' he said aloud to no one in particular.

'You may not have to get used to it,' said a dis-embodied voice in Elven.

His heart leapt beneath his ribs. He sat bolt upright. 'Who's there?' he said, scanning the darkness.

A hooded figure materialised out of the gloom before him. Tall and intimidating, the silhouette seemed impossibly darker than the unlit cell around it. And although Wread couldn't discern any iden-tifiable features beneath the cowl, the voice had sounded distinctly female.

'Who are you?' asked Wread.

'You would have known my name as Selenna, the Great Inquisitor.'

He pushed his back against the cell wall. Shock caught his mind. 'But you died fifty years ago … what are you doing here?'

'I am not so sure that I am dead, and as for being here … there is a power known only to the highest of Elves—*shifting* it is called—that allows us to move across great distances in an instant.'

He peered into the blackness of her face where he guessed her eyes would be. His mind raced as he tried to understand what the dead Inquisitor was doing here.

'You mean to teleport?' he said.

'Of sorts.'

He waited for the conversation to continue, but she remained silent. 'If you're not dead, then what are you?'

'Now *that* is the correct question. I am the means to exacting your revenge.'

Wread scoffed. 'I should have killed the Governor when I had the chance.'

'Choosing not to endanger your crew was an honourable decision, and one you should pride yourself for.'

'An honourable decision that landed me in prison. At least if I had killed him, it would have been worth it,' said Wread.

'The chance will come again,' she said.

'And how would you know?' said Wread, again scoffing.

Selenna took another step toward him. 'What if I told you that you're not limited to mastering one mancery but are capable of mastering them all—of bending every element to your will.'

'I would say you're insane,' said Wread, his brows knotting with annoyance. 'Every Elf knows that we can master only one mancery—fire, air, water, electricity or energy, that the Truthseers have no ability for mancery, and that the Lesser Races have no ability for either mancery or Truthseeing …'

'And what if I told you that everything you just said is wrong, and that the Elven King and his minions have hidden this knowledge?' she said.

'Why would they intentionally hold us back?'

'Why indeed,' she said, and although he couldn't see her face, he could hear the smile in her words.

For long seconds, Wread's breathing was the only sound that passed between them. His mind raced. Surely, it couldn't be true. Why would the King stop the Elves from accessing their full potential if they were able to command all elements with their mancery? And, yet … he knew he wouldn't be surprised if the Councils had kept secrets from the Elven population, especially if those secrets gave them more power, or the ability to travel vast distances in an instant. 'Clearly, you want something from me. What is it?'

'For now, I will simply say I want you to open your mind, Wreadallanon. Release yourself from the shackles of the Elven Councils and embrace the full potential of your own power. Learn to control all of the elements around you, and with that power, save Belissia *and* take your revenge.'

His reply was automatic, blurting before he'd a chance to consider her words. 'Save Belissia from what? The Humans?'

'Save Belissia from the Humans. Or save it from the Elven Councils.' She proffered two shadowed hands. 'Which would you prefer?'

'The Humans tortured and killed my brother,' said Wread. 'They wanted war before we gave them the reason to start it. They were just waiting for a chance to attack …'

'Now you're thinking. And are the Elves without fault?' When he offered no reply, she continued, 'Do you truly believe the Elves will save Belissia and protect the Lesser Races?'

'Protect them from what?' he asked, agitated at her ongoing questions.

'The Purge.'

'I don't believe the Purge is coming or that there is a great war ahead of us,' said Wredallanon.

'Well, time will prove one of us wrong.'